Tessa pu... fled the scre... Her legs felt weak and she grabbed a nearby chair to steady herself. She could taste bile in her throat. The candle had gone out when it hit the floor, but in the pale moonlight Tessa could see Sierra through the gauzy silken cocoon. Sierra's skin was gray, her cheeks were hollow, and her eyes were sunken. She looked unnaturally thin—emaciated.

Tessa stared at her for several long moments, hoping to see some movement, praying Sierra's chest would expand and contract with a breath. But Sierra was still.

Tessa felt her heart sink.

Her friend was dead.

**Read these other thrillers
available from HarperPaperbacks**

NIGHTMARE INN

THE ATTIC

T. S. Rue

HarperPaperbacks
A Division of HarperCollins*Publishers*

This is a work of fiction. The characters, incidents, and dialogues are products of the author's imagination and are not to be construed as real. Any resemblance to actual events or persons, living or dead, is entirely coincidental.

HarperPaperbacks   *A Division of* HarperCollins*Publishers*
10 East 53rd Street, New York, N.Y. 10022

Copyright © 1993 by Daniel Weiss Associates, Inc.
and Todd Strasser
Cover art copyright © 1993 Daniel Weiss Associates, Inc.

Produced by Daniel Weiss Associates, Inc.,
33 West 17th Street, New York, New York 10011.

First printing: September, 1993

Printed in the United States of America

HarperPaperbacks and colophon are trademarks of
HarperCollins*Publishers*

10 9 8 7 6 5 4 3 2 1

THE ATTIC

Chapter 1

As she stepped off the bus, Tessa Gilbert took a deep breath of the brisk fall air. It was late afternoon, and the sun had begun to set. The trees on the side of the road were just starting to change to their autumn colors, and the leaves were painted a fiery red by the sunset. Tessa smelled smoke in the air, and knew that someone nearby had started a fire in a wood-burning stove.

Brittany Graves, Sierra Gams, and Allie Burkhart followed Tessa off the bus. Brittany and Sierra were Tessa's two best friends. Brittany was a tall, slim redhead with angular looks and a brittle personality. Sierra had long, flowing black hair and softer looks, but she could be just as calculating as Brittany.

Tessa didn't know Allie very well. The small blonde had only recently moved to

Tessa's hometown. Tessa's mother worked in the same office as Allie's, and as a favor to Mrs. Burkhart, she'd asked Tessa to invite Allie along on their weekend trip to the New Arcadia Inn.

The bus roared away, leaving the girls and their bags on the side of the road.

"Where are we?" Brittany asked, looking around. She had her hands on her hips, and a grimace on her face.

Tessa suddenly realized they'd been stranded in the middle of nowhere. There were no houses and no people anywhere in sight. Both sides of the road were lined with thick woods. Far in the distance Tessa could see the rounded tops of small mountains.

"This has to be the right place. The bus driver wouldn't have dropped us here if it wasn't," Tessa replied.

"Well, I don't see anything that looks like a *place*, Tessa," Brittany said with a huff.

"Chill out, Brit," Sierra said. "It's pretty here. I mean, look at all those trees."

"The nature girl speaks," Brittany said, rolling her eyes.

"Knock it off, you guys," Tessa said. "You're giving me a major headache." Brittany and Sierra had been sniping at each other all day. Since the two girls were supposed to be such good friends, this behavior must have seemed

2

weird to Allie. But Tessa knew why her friends were mad at each other. She'd accidentally discovered the cause of their tension the night before.

"Did they give you any instructions on how to get to the resort?" Sierra asked Tessa.

Tessa shook her head. "Nope. All they said was to tell the bus driver to take us to the New Arcadia Inn. I figured the bus would stop right at the inn's front door."

"I just hope this place really exists," Brittany said.

"I once read a book about a hotel that was filled with ghosts," Allie suddenly volunteered.

Tessa and her friends looked at the small girl. Brittany frowned. Allie had barely talked during the long bus ride. Tessa had assumed Allie was just shy, but now she admitted to herself that there did seem to be something peculiar about Allie.

"What about it?" Sierra asked.

"Oh, nothing," Allie said. "It was filled with ghosts, that's all."

Brittany glanced at Tessa wryly. Her opinion of Allie was pretty obvious. Tessa thought Brittany was being a bit unfair. After all, they hardly knew Allie.

"So what are we going to do?" Sierra asked. "Wait here until someone comes for us?"

"I guess," Tessa said.

Sierra hugged herself and shivered a little. "Seems strange to me," she said.

"I think we should have gone to Loon Lake," Brittany said.

"We couldn't afford Loon Lake," Tessa said. "Remember? We couldn't afford to go anywhere until the New Arcadia gave us that great rate."

"Now I can see why they gave it to us," Brittany said, waving her hand around. "Not only are we in the middle of nowhere, but the New Arcadia doesn't even exist."

"Believe me, it exists," Tessa said. "Remember the picture of it on the brochure?"

"Then why do you think they gave us such a good rate?" Sierra asked.

"Probably because it's the end of the season," Tessa said.

"More like the end of the world," Brittany muttered.

"Will you lighten up?" Tessa asked. Sometimes Brittany's totally pessimistic attitude really got to her. "This is supposed to be a special weekend. Our parents let us go away on our own. It's just the three . . . uh . . . four of us. It's going to be a blast once we get there."

Allie had wandered a little way down the road and was staring up at something in a tall pine tree.

4

"I don't know how we're going to have a good time with her around," Brittany whispered.

"Give her a chance," Tessa whispered back. "Think about how you'd feel if you went away with three girls who were best friends and you hardly knew them. You'd feel pretty out of it too."

"I have a feeling Allie was out of it long before she met any of us," Brittany replied softly. "I mean, check her out. What's she looking at, anyway?"

The three girls turned in Allie's direction. She was still staring toward the top of the tree.

"Hey, Allie," Tessa called. "What're you looking at?"

Allie started walking back toward them. "I thought I saw something."

"Like what?" Sierra asked.

"Uh, some big black fuzzy thing," Allie said.

"Like a bear?" Tessa asked, alarmed.

"I couldn't tell," Allie said.

"Well, what happened to the big black fuzzy thing?" Brittany asked.

"It went away," Allie said.

Brittany rolled her eyes, and Sierra shook her head. Even Tessa was starting to worry that Allie might be too weird for them to deal with for a whole weekend. Once again Sierra hugged herself and shivered. Unlike the other girls, who were wearing jackets, she was wearing only a thin sweater.

"Look," Sierra said. "I really think we ought to do something. Like find a phone and call the place. It's getting cold, and in a couple of hours it's going to be dark. I really don't want to be—"

"Look!" Brittany gasped before Sierra could finish.

About fifty yards away, a man came out of the woods and onto the road. Tessa noticed something long and black dangling from his hand. The girls stepped close together in a nervous huddle.

"What's he carrying?" Brittany whispered.

"A whip," Allie whispered back.

The girls glanced at each other, wide-eyed.

The man was heading straight toward them.

Chapter 2

"One of you girls named Tessa Gilbert?" the man asked from about twenty feet away. He had long, silver-gray hair pulled back in a ponytail, and had turquoise and silver jewelry rings and bracelets on. He was wearing jeans, a denim shirt, and a leather vest. The thing in his hand looked like a long, black piece of cord with a metal clip on the end.

"I am," Tessa said nervously.

"Well, I'm Sebastian," the man said. "I came to bring you down to the inn. I guess these are your friends."

Tessa nodded. She supposed Sebastian had to be from the New Arcadia, or he wouldn't have known her name. "How do we get there?" she asked.

"There's a trail through the woods," Sebastian said, pointing back at the trees.

Tessa glanced at the others. This wasn't exactly the kind of welcome she'd expected. She was eager to get to the inn, but she didn't especially like the idea of going into the woods with a strange man.

"Isn't there any other way?" she asked.

"Well, we can stick to the road, but it'll take three times as long," Sebastian said.

"Come on, Tessa," Sierra said. "What are you scared of? It's only a bunch of trees and some squirrels. Nothing's going to get you."

"Although a big black fuzzy thing might," Brittany said with a wink.

Sebastian looked up. "What did you say?"

"Oh, uh, nothing," Brittany replied.

But Sebastian had heard her. "No, you said something about a black fuzzy thing."

"It was just a joke, really," Brittany explained.

The lines in Sebastian's face furrowed.

"Allie thought she saw something in a tree," Tessa said. "But when she tried to show us, it was gone."

"Oh, well, okay," Sebastian said, glancing back into the woods. "So, uh, shall I lead the way?"

Tessa looked questioningly at Sierra, who motioned her to follow Sebastian. Brittany just shrugged. If the other girls would go, she'd go too. Tessa didn't have to ask Allie. She was

8

already picking up her small suitcase, ready to head into the woods. But Tessa had to ask Sebastian a question first.

"Excuse me for being nosy," she said. "But what's that thing you're carrying?"

"This?" Sebastian held up the long black cord. "It's Fluffy's leash. She got out this morning, and I brought it along in case I found her."

So that explained it. Sebastian was looking for his dog, Fluffy.

Tessa and the other girls got their bags and followed Sebastian down the road and onto a trail through the woods.

"What happens if you don't find Fluffy?" Allie asked as they walked.

"Oh, I'm not worried much," Sebastian said. "She gets out all the time, but I always find her. Especially at this time of year."

"Why this time of year?" Sierra asked.

"Well, winter's coming and it's starting to get cold," Sebastian said. "Fluffy doesn't like the cold much. So, uh, I don't suppose any of you have ever stayed at the New Arcadia before, have you?"

The girls shook their heads.

"Well, I'm sure you're going to like it," Sebastian said. "It's usually really crowded at the inn, although there aren't too many people around right now, with the off-season and all. It's nice and quiet."

"What do you do for excitement?" Brittany asked.

"Don't you worry about that. There's always some of that at the New Arcadia," Sebastian replied.

A little while later they came out of the woods. The New Arcadia stood before them. It was an old, white, three-story inn that had been completely refurbished. Sebastian led them into the lobby filled with overstuffed chairs and couches. In one corner was a large stone fireplace. Several corridors led off from the lobby.

"This way, ladies," Sebastian said, bringing them toward the registration counter. A young woman with red hair was standing behind the counter.

"Sarah, could you check these nice young ladies in?" Sebastian asked. He turned to Tessa and the others. "Well, I've got to go out and find Fluffy. I hope you enjoy your stay."

Sarah went through a file and found their room forms. "You'll all be staying together in room 318," she said. "You've got two king-size beds. And don't forget that dinner is at seven tonight in the dining room."

"You better believe I won't forget," Brittany said. "I'm starving."

A good-looking guy wearing a brown bell-boy's uniform appeared. He had wavy chest-nut-colored hair, dark blue eyes, and a shy smile.

"Nick, please take their bags to room 318," Sarah said.

"Right this way," Nick said, picking up the bags. He carried their bags up to the room with the girls following behind. Brittany kept winking at Tessa and making motions as if she wanted to grab Nick from behind. Nick let them into the room. It was fairly large, with the two beds and a window that looked out toward the front of the inn.

Nick put down the bags and brushed his hair out of his eyes. "If there's anything you need, just buzz the front desk," he said.

"I need something," Brittany said with a flirtatious smile. "I need to know what time you get off work tonight."

Sierra glanced at Tessa and rolled her eyes. Nick grinned shyly back at Brittany.

"Well, to tell you the truth," he said, "I work pretty late tonight."

"How late?" Brittany asked. Tessa couldn't believe how forward her friend was being.

"Well, it depends on whether more guests arrive, and at what time," Nick said. "Sometimes I'm on as late as two in the morning."

"Well, if by some chance you get off early

tonight, why don't you come by and see if we're still up?" Brittany suggested.

"Okay," Nick said with a smile. "Maybe I will."

He went out and closed the door behind him.

"Maybe we'll have some excitement after all," Brittany said, turning to the other girls and smiling.

But Sierra didn't look amused. "I really don't understand you," she said. "Remember your boyfriend, Andrew? What if he found out?"

Brittany stared daggers at Sierra. "Knowing you, you'd probably tell him," she snapped.

"Maybe I would," Sierra shot back.

"Boy, some friend," Brittany muttered, shaking her head.

"You get what you deserve," Sierra said.

Tessa knew she had to intervene before a real fight broke out. "Look, can we please not have a fight?" she asked. "We came here to have a fun-filled weekend, remember?"

Brittany and Sierra glared at each other, then started to unpack their bags. Tessa started to unpack hers also. She and Sierra both knew that Brittany often flirted with other guys behind Andrew's back. Even though they thought it was pretty low of her, they usually just shook their heads and didn't give Brittany grief about it.

But something had changed between Sierra and Brittany, and Tessa knew what it was.

The day before, Tessa had stayed late after school to finish an art project. She was running out the door to catch the last bus when she suddenly remembered she'd forgotten an important book. She'd dashed back to her locker.

As Tessa came around the corner and headed for her locker, she saw two people standing in front of a locker halfway down the hall. They were locked in an embrace. Tessa stopped, not wanting to disturb them. The kiss lasted a long time, and when they parted, Tessa had the shock of her life. It was Brittany's boyfriend, Andrew, and Sierra!

Tessa had hidden in a doorway until they'd gone. Then she'd gotten her book.

From that second on, Tessa had dreaded going away for the weekend with Brittany and Sierra. In a way, she was almost glad Allie had come along, if for no other reason than that it might help keep Sierra and Brittany on good behavior. Tessa still didn't know if, or what, Brittany knew about Sierra and Andrew, but it was obvious she'd begun to suspect something.

Tessa took her makeup bag and toiletries out of her suitcase and took them into the bathroom. She flicked the light on and was placing her things on the counter when she happened to glance into the mirror.

There she saw something that chilled her to her bones.

Her makeup bag fell to the floor.

"*Ahhhhhhh!*" A scream tore out of her throat.

14

Chapter 3

"*Ahhhhhhh!*" Tessa screamed again.

"What is it?" Brittany gasped, rushing into the bathroom. Tessa staggered out to the bed and sat down to catch her breath. Her heart was pounding and her chest felt tight.

"What happened?" Sierra asked, a quaver in her voice. Her eyes darted toward the bathroom.

"I . . ." Tessa choked on the words.

"There's nothing in there," Brittany said, stepping back into the room.

Tessa suddenly felt a bit silly. "I saw a spider," she admitted.

"A spider?" Brittany frowned. "Is that all?"

It was hard to explain. Tessa considered herself a fairly coolheaded and rational person. But the one thing that she was absolutely terrified of was spiders. For as long as she could remember, she'd been scared to death of the creepy little monsters.

"I really can't stand them," Tessa said, still shaking despite herself. "Besides, it was pulling these little sacks behind it." The memory sent shivers down her spine.

"Sacks?" Brittany wrinkled her nose in disgust.

"They were probably egg sacks," Sierra guessed.

"Or food for the winter," Allie said. Maybe it was because it sounded so weird, or because Allie didn't speak much, but the other girls stared at her.

"Food?" Sierra made a face. "Gross!"

"Winter's coming," Allie said. "All the insects a spider normally feeds on will soon be gone. It has to store up, or else it'll die."

"Insects for food . . . Yuck!" Brittany shivered.

"She sucks their juices," Allie said nonchalantly.

The thought made Tessa feel ill. "Please stop talking about it, Allie," she said. "You're going to make me sick."

"What did you mean, *she?*" Brittany asked. "How do you know the spider's a *her?*"

"I don't know," Allie replied with a shrug. "It just feels like a she."

"*Feels like a she?*" Brittany rolled her eyes.

"Do you think it's still in there?" Sierra asked.

"I don't know," Tessa said. "Why don't you go look?"

Sierra stuck her head into the doorway. After a few moments she turned back at Tessa. "You were scared of *that*?"

Now Brittany got up and returned to the bathroom. "Tessa, it's tiny. I didn't even notice it before." Brittany went to her suitcase and took out a shoe.

"What are you going to do?" Tessa asked.

"I'm going to squash it, what else?" Brittany replied, heading back toward the bathroom.

"No, you're not," Sierra said, blocking her path.

"What's with you?" Brittany asked.

"It's a living creature," Sierra said. "It might have babies to take care of. Besides, it never did anything to you."

"It scared Tessa pretty badly," Brittany said.

"Actually, *it* didn't do anything," Sierra said. "Tessa saw it and got scared. All the spider's doing is going on with its life."

"Nature Girl speaks again." Brittany shook her head and sighed. "Get out of the way, Sierra. I really need to use the bathroom, and I can't until that spider's squashed and flushed."

Sierra stood in the bathroom doorway and shook her head. "I'm not going to let you do it."

Brittany tossed the shoe onto the bed. "Okay, great, Sierra. We'll let the spider live in the bathroom. Meanwhile none of us will be able to go in there. Does that make you happy?"

"All we have to do is move it," Allie said.

Again, the other girls stared at her.

"You mean, touch it?" Brittany asked, clearly revolted by the thought.

"Well, we don't have to pick it up with our fingers," Allie said.

"She's right," Sierra said. "Maybe we could get it to crawl onto something, and then we could carry it outside."

Allie went over to the desk and picked up a room-service menu. "I bet we could use this."

Tessa jumped up from the bed and headed for the door. "I'm out of here. Let me know when our visitor has left."

"I'll go with you," Brittany said.

The girls left the room and walked down the corridor, then took the elevator to the lobby. The red-haired girl named Sarah was standing behind the front desk, but the rest of the lobby was empty. Outside, it was rapidly getting dark. A fire was burning in the big stone fireplace.

"Want to go for a walk outside?" Tessa asked.

"Why don't we sit by the fire instead?" Brittany suggested.

"Okay," Tessa agreed.

The girls walked over to the fireplace and sat down on a long couch. For a moment they stared at the bright orange and yellow flames leaping off the burning logs.

"Allie gives me the creeps," Brittany said. "She's totally bizarre."

"Oh, I don't know," Tessa said. "I mean, she came up with a logical suggestion for dealing with the spider."

Brittany stared at her. "Don't tell me you think she's normal."

"Well, I wouldn't go *that* far," Tessa joked.

"Why did she have to come with us, anyway?"

"I told you," Tessa said. "My mother works with her mother. Allie's new in town, and her mother asked my mother if I would do something with her."

"It's not like you," Brittany said. "There are lots of other things you could have done with her. You two could have gone to a movie or to the mall. You didn't have to invite her to go away for the weekend with us."

Tessa knew that was true.

"So?" Brittany said.

19

"So, what?" Tessa replied.

"You're not fooling me, Tessa," Brittany said.

"Okay," Tessa said with a sigh. "I couldn't help noticing that you and Sierra aren't getting along lately. I thought if I invited Allie, things wouldn't be . . . so intense."

Brittany nodded, but didn't say anything for a moment. She glanced over the back of the couch at the empty lobby, then turned and looked at Tessa.

"I think Sierra likes Andrew," Brittany said.

"You do?" Tessa asked, pretending to act surprised.

"You know, she's always been jealous of me," Brittany went on. "It would be like her to try to steal my boyfriend. Besides, I've heard rumors."

"About what?" Tessa asked.

Brittany shrugged and didn't answer.

"What makes you think she likes Andrew?" Tessa asked.

"You mean, besides the rumors?" Brittany asked.

"People make up rumors all the time," Tessa said. "That doesn't mean they're true."

"Well, it's also a feeling I get," Brittany said. "It's the way she looks at him when we're all together, and the way she always asks me

20

about him." Brittany looked over the back of the couch again.

"What are you looking for?" Tessa asked.

"Oh, nothing," Brittany said.

"Nick?" Tessa guessed.

Brittany smiled. "He is cute, don't you think?"

"I think I don't understand how one second you can be upset because you think Sierra's trying to steal your boyfriend," Tessa said, "and in the next second you're looking around for Nick."

"If something happened with Nick, it wouldn't be a big deal," Brittany said. "I just want to have some fun this weekend."

"That doesn't seem unfair to you?" Tessa asked.

"No," Brittany said. She turned again and looked over the back of the couch. This time she didn't turn back. Tessa saw that Brittany was looking at Allie, carrying a plastic cup with the room-service menu covering the top.

Tessa shivered as she realized that the spider must be inside the cup. She watched Allie go out the front door.

"She is one strange girl," Brittany muttered.

"Maybe," Tessa said, getting up. "But at least we can go back to the room now."

* * *

21

Back in the room, Tessa, Sierra, and Brittany continued to unpack in silence. The tension between her two friends was almost unbearable to Tessa. She was relieved when Allie finally returned from outside.

"Did you find a good home for your pal?" Brittany asked.

"I didn't take it too far from the inn," Allie said. "I know it will want to come back inside when it starts to get colder."

"What a reassuring thought," Brittany cracked.

"How would you like it if someone threw *you* outside in the middle of the winter?" Sierra asked.

"I think there's a big difference between me and a spider," Brittany said.

"Less than you might think," Sierra shot back.

"Thanks for the compliment, Sierra," Brittany said. "What's with you, anyway?"

Tessa could see another potential fight erupting. "Will you guys please stop it? You're driving me crazy."

"No, wait," Brittany said, glaring at Sierra. "I'd really like to know what Sierra meant by that remark."

"All I meant is that you're both living creatures," Sierra said innocently. "There's no more reason to squash a spider than there is to squash you. Actually, spiders do a lot of good."

"Oh, of course," Brittany said.

"They kill a lot of annoying insects," Sierra explained. "Like mosquitoes and lice."

"Well, thank you for this enlightening nature lesson, Sierra," Brittany said sarcastically. "I truly feel like I am now one with the environment."

"I don't know why you always have to act so cool," Sierra said. "The environment's important. It wouldn't hurt if you cared about it."

"Can we please talk about something else?" Tessa asked. "I'm really not interested in hearing you two argue, and all this talk about spiders is making me sick."

Sierra and Brittany were quiet after that. Tessa finished unpacking and went into the bathroom to wash up for dinner. She carefully looked in all the corners, behind the toilet, and inside the vanity. Satisfied that there were no more spiders in the bathroom, she washed her face and brushed her shoulder-length, light-brown hair.

As an afterthought, she put on a little makeup. She really hadn't come to the New Arcadia expecting to meet anyone, but now she sort of hoped that she would. Finding some guys to hang around with might be a good diversion from the minor war brewing between her two best friends.

As she left the bathroom Tessa glanced out the small window. It was completely dark now, but the moon was out. In the distance, barely illuminated by moonlight, she could see what looked like a man walking a medium-size dog. Tessa smiled to herself. Sebastian must have found Fluffy.

Soon the girls left the room and walked down the hall to the elevator. Sierra pushed the down button and they waited for the elevator to come. Suddenly Tessa heard a strange sound, as if some animal was scampering on the floor above them.

"Did you hear that?" she asked.

"What?" Sierra asked.

"Listen," Tessa said. The girls listened. Soon Tessa heard the scampering sound again.

"Sounds like something's in the attic," Sierra said. "We used to have squirrels in our attic at home. They made sounds like that."

Tessa nodded and turned back to the elevator. It still hadn't come.

"What's taking it so long?" Brittany asked.

"Maybe it has to stop on the other floors," Allie said.

"For who?" Brittany asked. "This place is totally deserted. And there are only three floors, anyway."

Once again Tessa heard the scampering sound above them. Only now it seemed louder and was coming toward them. The girls grew silent and looked up at the ceiling.

The scampering sound was growing louder. It sounded like heavy rain on a roof. Suddenly the running paws seemed to pass right over them and then go away, once again growing distant.

"That's some squirrel," Brittany said.

"Maybe it's a raccoon," Sierra said.

"It sounded like more than one," Tessa said.

"Maybe it's two raccoons doing wind sprints," Allie said.

Tessa glanced back at the elevator. "It really should have been here by now," she said, pushing the down button again.

"Well, if it doesn't come we can stand here and listen to the thing in the attic all night long," Sierra said. "That would be a real blast."

"Listen," Brittany said, "I'm so hungry that if the elevator doesn't come soon I may go up there and *eat* the thing in the attic."

Tessa had to smile. That was the Brittany she liked. The one who cracked jokes and made them all laugh.

"I think we better find the stairs and walk down," Sierra said, pointing toward the far end of the hall at a red EXIT sign. "I wouldn't want to see Brittany munching on a rodent."

"Why don't we use the stairway near our room?" Tessa asked. There was another red EXIT sign next door to their room.

"The one down the hall's closer to the lobby," Sierra said. "And that means it will be closer to the dining room."

She had a point, and the girls started away from the elevator. As they walked, Tessa listened again for the scampering sounds above them, but didn't hear anything.

Tessa reached the exit door first and went through. The other girls followed her. As soon as she'd entered the stairway, Tessa suddenly stopped.

"Don't let the door—" she started to say.

Click! She was too late. Behind them the exit door swung shut.

They were standing in pitch-black darkness.

Chapter 4

"Oh no!" Brittany gasped.

"Stay calm," Tessa said quickly. "And don't move. You don't want to push someone down the stairs by accident."

"What are we going to do?" Sierra asked.

"Find a light switch," Tessa said, tracing the cold cinder-block wall with her fingers.

"Any luck?" Brittany asked.

"Not yet." Tessa searched the walls on both sides of the door where a light switch should have been, but found nothing.

"Well?" Brittany asked in the dark.

"No luck," Tessa said. "I can't find the switch."

"Why aren't there any lights?" Sierra asked.

"I guess that's the million-dollar question, isn't it?" Brittany replied.

"Can someone feel for the doorknob?" Tessa asked.

"I can," Sierra said. "Darn, it's locked."

"Great," Brittany muttered. "I love being stuck on the stairs when it's so dark I can't see my nose in front of my face."

"It's cold," Allie said.

The girls became quiet. Tessa realized Allie was right. It *was* cold. Very cold! Tessa hugged herself. She could hear a faint clattering sound.

"What's that sound?" Sierra asked.

"It's me," Allie said, her voice no more than a whisper. "My teeth are chattering."

Tessa had also started to shiver. "Is it my imagination, or is it actually colder in here than it was outside?" she asked.

"It feels that way," Brittany said.

"Maybe it's because we've been in a warm room for a while," Sierra said.

"You know what?" Brittany said. "I don't really care if it's colder in here than outside. I just want to go downstairs and get out of here. This scene is a little too dull for me."

"Okay," Tessa said, taking a tentative step. "I saw a metal rail right before the door closed. I'm going to try to find it and go down."

Tessa reached out into the dark. It was an eerie feeling. She couldn't see a thing, and it felt as if she was reaching into pure nothingness. She was afraid she was going to lose her balance, slip off a step, and tumble down the stairs. Finally she felt the metal railing. It was freezing, almost as cold as an ice tray in her freezer. Still, Tessa gripped it tightly and took a step forward. Her foot touched the next step.

"Okay, I found the rail," she said. "Everyone follow me. And make sure you hold on tightly."

Slowly and carefully, Tessa walked down the stairs. Finally as she turned a corner she could see the vaguest hint of light seeping out from the exit door on what must have been the second floor. Tessa stepped onto the landing and felt for the doorknob.

She found it, and twisted hard. It wouldn't open.

"I can't believe it," she muttered.

"What now?" Brittany asked through chattering teeth.

"This door's locked too."

"Oh, great!" Brittany said. "What if all of them are locked?"

"We'll be stuck in here forever," Sierra gasped. "We'll freeze to death!"

"Will you please chill out?" Tessa snapped.

"We're *all* chilling out, Tessa," Brittany replied. "That's the problem."

"Maybe the light switch is here," Allie said.

"Good idea," Tessa said. Tessa felt around the door frame again. But there was no switch.

"I don't get it," she said.

"What do we do now?" Brittany asked. "Maybe we should pray. That's what they always do on TV."

Tessa smiled in the dark for an instant. "Okay, look," she said. "There's no reason to panic. We'll keep going down. One of the doors is bound to be open."

"And if it isn't?" Sierra asked.

"I don't know," Tessa replied. "We'll worry about it then."

They worked their way to the first floor, but the door there was also locked.

"I'm really getting a bad feeling about this," Sierra said, her voice trembling with fear.

"I'm really getting a *cold* feeling from this," Brittany added.

"The next floor is the lobby," Tessa said. "If any door is going to be open, it's that one."

Still holding the freezing railing, she started down the dark steps again.

"I hope you're right," Sierra said as she followed.

It occurred to Tessa that she hadn't heard a word from Allie since the third floor.

"Allie?" she called.

There was no answer. Tessa stopped and looked back up the stairs. She couldn't see anything except pure darkness.

"Allie?" she called again.

"I'm here," Allie replied. But her voice was hardly more than a whimper.

"Are you okay?" Tessa asked.

"I'm so cold," Allie replied. Unlike the others who were simply complaining about the cold, she sounded as if she was really suffering from it.

"Just hang on," Tessa said. "We're going to be in the lobby in a second."

Once again Tessa could see light coming from under a door. She felt her heart begin to beat harder, and she bit her lip nervously. The door to the lobby had to be open. It just *had* to be! Tessa stepped on the landing and reached for the doorknob.

It didn't turn.

"Darn it!" she muttered.

"What's wrong?" Sierra asked behind her.

"It's locked."

"Then we're really trapped," Sierra gasped, her voice etched with fear.

"What are we going to do?" Brittany cried frantically.

"Calm down, Brit," Tessa said.

"Calm down!" Brittany snapped irritably. "That's easy for you to say, Tessa, but it doesn't change the fact that we're trapped in here in the dark, freezing to death."

"I know," Tessa snapped back, feeling scared and pretty irritable herself. "Just let me

31

think for a second. There has to be a way out of here."

"You can go ahead and think all you want," Sierra said. "But I know what I'm going to do."

The next thing Tessa knew, Sierra had pushed past her and started to bang on the exit door to the lobby with her fists. "Hey!" she shouted. "Can anyone hear me? We're stuck in here! Please let us out!"

Now Tessa heard two sets of fists as Brittany joined Sierra at the door.

"Help!" Brittany yelled. "Let us out!"

The girls banged on the door a few more times.

"All right!" Sierra suddenly exclaimed.

"What is it?" Tessa asked in the dark.

"The doorknob's turning," Sierra said.

She and Brittany stopped banging on the door and waited in silence. Tessa heard a faint *click-clack*. Someone was finally letting them out!

They waited a second more, but all they heard were the sounds of their own breathing.

"What happened?" Tessa whispered.

"I don't know," Sierra whispered back. "I'm sure someone tried to turn the doorknob from the other side."

Tessa quickly felt her way past Sierra and grabbed the doorknob. She turned as hard as

32

she could, but the knob didn't budge.

"It's still locked," Tessa said.

Sierra and Brittany both started banging on the door and shouting for help again.

"Hey, don't go away!" Sierra shouted.

"Come back!" Brittany cried. "We're still stuck in here!"

They banged a little longer, but there was no response from the other side.

"I can't believe they'd leave us in here," Brittany cried.

"Maybe they went for a key or something," Sierra said.

"What good is an exit door that's locked on both sides?" Brittany asked.

"You're right," Sierra said. "It's crazy."

Once again, the girls started to bang on the door. Tessa hoped it would attract help, but she wasn't about to leave it up to them.

Tessa could feel a cold draft coming from below them. Maybe there was another way out. Maybe the steps went down yet another flight—to a basement or something.

Brittany and Sierra continued to pound on the door and shout for help. But it had been a while since Tessa had heard Allie's voice.

"Allie," she said over the commotion. "Are you still here?"

"Yes."

The sound of Allie's voice startled Tessa.

33

She must have been standing right next to Tessa. It was so dark, though, Tessa couldn't even see her.

"Just wanted to make sure you were still with us," Tessa said. She realized she'd started to feel protective of the girl, the way an older sister might feel.

"I am, but I'm really, really cold," Allie said.

"Well, hopefully we'll be out of here in a few minutes," Tessa said.

"Can I help?" Allie asked.

"Well, I don't know," Tessa said. "I'm not so sure what to do either. I was thinking of going down a little farther. Maybe we can get out through the basement."

She turned and stared into the blackness. Behind her Brittany and Sierra were still banging and screaming. Tessa remembered how empty the lobby had been earlier in the evening. Her friends might bang and shout for hours without being heard. Tessa felt for the rail again. She was sure the basement was the answer. She found the railing and took a step down.

"Nooooooo!"

Tessa screamed as she stepped into thin cold air! There was no step below her—she was plummeting into the black nothingness!

Chapter 5

"*Help me! Help!*" Tessa clung for life to the icy railing. Her feet kicked desperately beneath her.

"*Help!*" she screamed again.

"*Hey, we're stuck in here! Help us!*" Brittany and Sierra were still screaming themselves. They either didn't hear her or must have thought she was screaming with them.

"*Help!*" Tessa screamed once more. She was starting to panic. Her grip on the railing was slipping. In a moment she was going to plunge into the icy void below.

"Tessa?" a voice asked. It was Allie.

"Allie!" Tessa gasped. "You have to help me. Get Brittany and Sierra."

"What's wrong?" Allie asked.

"I don't have time to explain," Tessa gasped. "Just get them. Hurry!"

She listened while Allie got Brittany's and Sierra's attention. Her heart was beating madly with adrenaline and fear.

"Tessa, where are you?" Sierra asked.

"Right in front of you," Tessa said. "Be careful. There's no stairs. It's just air. I'm hanging on to the rail."

"What do you want us to do?" Brittany asked.

"Help me," Tessa gasped. "I'm slipping. If I fall I don't know how far down it is. Pull me back up."

For a second, Tessa could see and hear nothing.

"I'll do it," Allie said in the dark.

"I'll hold you," Sierra said. "Brittany, you hold me."

"Please hurry!" Tessa cried as her hands slid a tiny bit on the icy rail.

Suddenly Tessa felt Allie grab her wrist and squeeze tight. It wasn't enough to pull her up, but it was enough to stop her from sliding any farther.

"Do you have her?" Sierra asked.

"Yes," Allie said. "Everyone pull."

Slowly Tessa felt the pressure on her wrist increase. She was able to start inching herself upward along the railing.

"Keep pulling!" she urged. "It's working!"

(Allie continued to hold her wrist.) Tessa

was gradually able to climb up the railing. Finally her foot touched the concrete landing and she heaved herself forward to safety.

The girls staggered backward onto the cold concrete floor and stood there exhausted for a few moments. Tessa felt weak with relief.

"Are you okay?" Allie asked.

"Yes," Tessa gasped. "I am. Thank you. You saved my life."

"Temporarily," Brittany muttered. "If we don't get out of here soon, we're all going to freeze to death."

"She's right," Sierra said. Together the girls started banging on the door and shouting again. Tessa knew she should join them, but she was still recovering from her near fall.

"Wait!" Sierra suddenly said. "Did you hear something?"

The girls instantly became quiet. On the other side of the door a voice said, "Is someone in there?"

"*Yes!*" they all cried at once.

The next thing Tessa knew, the doorknob began to turn. Then the door opened a crack and the landing was illuminated with dull light. The other girls were staring out, but Tessa looked back at the empty cold space the staircase disappeared into. There was nothing there.

"What are you doing in here?" a male voice asked.

Tessa turned and saw Nick standing in the doorway.

"It's a long story," Brittany replied, "but boy, are we glad to see you."

The girls stepped into the lobby, squinting as their eyes adjusted to the bright overhead lights. Brittany and Sierra were still hugging themselves and shivering. Tessa's fingers and toes felt numb, and her ears began to burn as they warmed up. But Allie appeared to have suffered the most. Her teeth chattered uncontrollably and her skin was even paler than usual. Her thin lips were blue.

"Are you okay?" Tessa asked her.

"I think so," Allie said in a voice that was just above a whisper. "I just need to warm up."

Meanwhile Nick was staring at them with a puzzled expression on his face. "What were you doing in the stairwell?"

"The elevator wouldn't come," Sierra explained. "So we decided to walk down."

"What do you mean, the elevator wouldn't come?" Nick questioned.

"I mean, we pushed the button and waited forever, but it didn't come," Sierra said.

"That's weird," Nick said. "You guys are staying on the third floor, right?"

The girls nodded.

38

"I took the elevator down from there not two minutes ago," Nick said. "It came right away."

Tessa and the other girls gazed at each other in wonder. Then Brittany turned back to Nick.

"Why are all the doors in the stairwell locked?" she asked.

"They're not supposed to be," Nick said. "This is an emergency exit."

"Well, believe me, the doors are locked," Brittany said.

"And there are no lights," Sierra added.

"No lights?" Nick frowned.

"Forget the doors and the lights," Tessa said. "There's no *stairs*. I took a step toward the basement and almost fell into thin air."

Nick looked as though he didn't believe them. He started to reach for the exit door.

"Uh, Nick!"

The girls turned to see Sebastian walking toward them from across the lobby.

"Yes?" Nick said, pausing.

Sebastian pointed at the elevator. The doors had just opened and a man and a woman came out, each lugging two heavy bags. "Could you please help them to their car?"

"Of course." Nick quickly hustled to the departing guests.

Sebastian smiled at the girls. "So, I assume you've come for dinner."

"Well, yes," Tessa said. "But—"

"It's being served right now," Sebastian said, interrupting her. "You really should hurry to the dining room."

"Sounds good to me," Brittany started across the lobby.

"Enjoy," Sebastian said, and strolled toward the front desk.

"Brittany!" Tessa gasped as she and the others hurried to catch up with her.

"What?" Brittany asked.

"What's wrong with you?" Tessa asked. "We were just trapped in the stairwell. It was locked and there were no lights. It was unbelievably cold and I practically fell to my death. Doesn't that mean anything to you?"

Brittany rolled her eyes. "Look, Tessa, are you still in the stairwell?"

"Obviously not," Tessa replied.

"Did you live?"

"What are you talking about?" Tessa asked. "Of course."

"Are you still cold?" Brittany asked.

"No."

"Are you hungry?"

Tessa had to admit that her stomach was grumbling. "Well, yes."

"I rest my case." Brittany turned and

started to march toward the dining room again.

Tessa looked at Sierra in disbelief.

"Wait until she's had something to eat," Sierra advised. "*Then* try talking to her."

Tessa immediately noticed that the inn's dining room was almost empty. Two elderly couples sat at one table, and some people in black and white uniforms sat at another. Tessa assumed they were employees of the New Arcadia. Brittany was already making her way along the buffet table, heaping food onto her plate.

"Wow, this place really is empty," Sierra said.

"Yeah, I wonder why Sebastian told us to hurry?" Tessa asked.

Neither Sierra nor Allie had an answer. The three girls walked over to the buffet tables, got plates, and started to select food. A few moments later they joined Brittany at a table. Brittany was wolfing down a plate filled with chicken, mashed potatoes, and peas.

As Tessa sat down, she glanced at Allie's plate. The small girl had taken only one chicken wing and a single slice of bread for herself.

"You sure that's enough?" Tessa asked her.

"I never eat much," Allie replied. Her teeth had stopped chattering and her lips had

41

returned to their normal color.

"Good, then you can leave more for Miss Piglet," Sierra said.

Brittany glared at her. "Well, excuse me for having a healthy appetite," she huffed.

Once again Tessa felt the need to mediate. "It does seem like an awful lot of food, Brit."

"It's the first thing I've had to eat all day," Brittany said. "We got on the bus before lunchtime, remember?"

"Why didn't you have breakfast?" Allie asked.

"Because I heard a rumor last night that made me lose my appetite," Brittany said, staring at Sierra.

Sierra glanced down at her plate and didn't say anything.

Now Tessa knew it was time to change the topic of conversation. "I can't believe we're all sitting here acting like we've forgotten what happened to us less than ten minutes ago," she said.

"Tessa's right," Sierra said. "It was kind of weird."

"What was so weird about it?" Brittany asked.

"Well, a stairwell with no lights and all the doors locked," Sierra said.

"It probably has lights," Brittany said. "We just couldn't find them."

"But it was so cold," Allie said. She seemed to be shivering at the memory.

"Well, maybe there was a door to the outside open somewhere," Brittany said.

"That might be so, but how do you explain the fact that the staircase ended in thin air?" Tessa asked. "I mean, I really think I could have been killed if Allie hadn't saved me."

"I thought we all saved you," Sierra said.

"You're right," Tessa said.

"But you really couldn't see what was down there," Brittany said. "I mean, for all you know, you just missed a step."

Tessa shook her head. "Believe me, there was *nothing* down there. I could feel it."

"Look, Tessa," Brittany said. "Why would they have a staircase that ended with nothing? It doesn't make any sense."

"Maybe you should ask him," Sierra said, pointing behind them.

Tessa and Brittany turned around and saw Sebastian coming toward them.

"So, how's dinner?" he asked. "Is everything all right?"

"Yes," Sierra said. "But Tessa has a question for you."

Sebastian turned and gazed at Tessa, who suddenly felt shy. "What is it, Tessa?"

"Well, uh, before, when we were stuck in that stairwell, I tried to go down to the base-

43

ment, but there was nothing there. I mean, there was a stairway, there just weren't any steps on it," Tessa explained.

"There is no basement," Sebastian said with a frown.

"Well, there must be something down there," Tessa said.

"Yes, there's supposed to be a wooden barrier," Sebastian said evasively. "We put it there to prevent anyone from falling. Maybe it broke. I'll have to check."

Brittany gave Tessa a smile that said *I told you so*. But Tessa had other questions.

"Why was it so cold in the stairwell?" she asked. "And why couldn't we find the light switch?"

"Well, that's easy," Sebastian replied. "The lights are operated from a master switch in the lobby. Someone must have accidentally shut them off. And the reason it was so cold is that the stairwell goes clear up to the roof. People are always going up there and leaving the door open."

"But it felt much colder than it is outside," Sierra said.

"Oh, well, I don't know about that," Sebastian said. "The temperature's dropped quite a bit in the past few hours. I think you'd be pretty surprised if you went outside right now." Sebastian gave them a satisfied grin.

"So, ladies, have I answered all your questions?"

"I have one more," Brittany said. "How come it's so dead around here?"

Sebastian's eyebrows rose. "Dead, did you say?"

"I meant, how come it's so empty?" Brittany said. "Where is everyone?"

"Oh, well, it's the end of the season," Sebastian said. "We never get that many people around this time of year. That's why you got such a good deal on your weekend package."

"We weren't the only people who got it, were we?" Sierra asked.

"Oh, no," Sebastian said. "In fact, we're expecting a whole bunch of guests tomorrow. We get quiet nights like this every once in a while. Anyway, I hope you enjoy your stay, and if you have any more questions, please feel free to ask."

He started to turn away. Suddenly Allie looked up. "I have a question."

Sebastian turned back and scowled. Brittany glanced at Tessa and rolled her eyes.

"I really should be going," Sebastian said.

"What are those noises we heard in the attic?" Allie asked, as if she hadn't heard him.

For a moment Sebastian stared at her. His whole expression had changed. No longer did he look congenial and friendly. His eyes narrowed and his lips were pressed tightly together. Tessa was afraid Allie had made him angry.

"The attic, did you say?"

The girls nodded.

"Whatever you do," he warned, "don't go in the attic."

Chapter 6

The girls glanced nervously at each other.

"Uh, she didn't say anything about *going* into the attic," Sierra said. "She was just wondering what was making those sounds."

"What sounds?" Sebastian asked.

"Well, they were like animal sounds," Sierra said. "Like something is running around up there."

"Something *big*," Allie added.

"Well, I'll ask someone to take a look at it," Sebastian said, sounding very serious. "In the meantime, remember, the attic is strictly off-limits to guests. There's no reason for you to go up there. *Ever*."

The next thing the girls knew, he had walked away and left the dining room. Tessa and the other girls stared at each other, wide-eyed.

"Wow, what was *that* all about?" Brittany asked.

"I don't know," Sierra replied with a grin. "Maybe there are ghosts up there or something. What do *you* think, Allie?"

Allie shook her head as if she was taking the question very seriously. "I didn't think ghosts could have footsteps. Maybe people leave their dogs up there."

Brittany twisted her face with false fright. "Maybe it's dog ghosts! The ghosts of all the dogs that ever lived here."

"The ghosts of Fluffy's ancestors," Sierra added with a smile of her own.

"Maybe we should go see," Allie suggested.

Brittany gave her a look. "Be my guest."

"Aren't you curious?" Allie asked.

"It really sounded like he didn't want us to go up there," Tessa reminded her.

Allie nodded and looked a little disappointed. "You're right."

Brittany had a devilish look on her face. "Of course, Allie, if you *do* decide to go up and see, I'm sure the rest of us would promise never to tell Sebastian you did."

"Now, don't give the girl ideas," Sierra said, wagging her finger at Brittany.

Tessa realized Allie was giving her a questioning look. "If you want my advice," Tessa said, "I wouldn't."

"Oh, boo hoo," Brittany pretended to sniff. "Tessa's always ruining our fun."

"If you're so curious," Tessa said, "why don't *you* go up there?"

"No, thanks," Brittany replied.

The girls finished their dinners and headed back out to the lobby. For the moment, Brittany and Sierra appeared to have forgotten their animosity toward each other. They kept laughing and making jokes about the ghosts in the attic. Even Allie had started to smile.

Sierra walked up to the elevator and pushed the button. "Let's see what happens *this* time," she said.

"Well, whatever happens, I for one am *not* going back up those stairs," Brittany said.

"Oh? Don't you like being locked in the frozen dark?" Sierra asked jokingly. "I hear it's simply wonderful for the complexion."

"Yes," Brittany agreed. "I hear it scares the pimples right off your face."

"Maybe *that's* what's in the attic!" Allie broke in. "Hundreds of pimples live up there, waiting for one of us to come up, so they can latch on."

Brittany and Sierra suddenly stopped their banter and got extremely quiet. They both stared at Allie.

"That has to be one of the more bizarre

statements I've ever heard," Brittany replied after a moment.

Tessa saw the slightest bit of color rise in Allie's face as she realized she'd made a fool of herself. Once again Tessa felt the desire to protect her.

"Well," she said, "I thought it was kind of funny."

"Tessa to the rescue," Brittany muttered.

Allie glanced at Tessa and smiled appreciatively.

A second later the elevator doors opened and the girls got in.

"Next stop, third floor," Sierra announced. "Swimwear, dog ghosts, and swarms of pimples. Please step back and let the doors close."

The girls were silent during the brief trip to the third door. Tessa held her breath, almost expecting to get trapped in the elevator. When the doors opened, Brittany and Sierra tiptoed out as if they were entering enemy territory.

"See anything strange?" Brittany asked, making her eyes wide.

"Hear anything peculiar?" Sierra asked.

They stood stock-still.

No one heard a thing.

"I guess we're safe," Brittany whispered.

Suddenly a terrible screech ripped through the air.

"*What was that!?*" Brittany gasped as she and Sierra huddled together. Without realizing it, Tessa stepped close to Allie and took her hand. The smaller girl squeezed Tessa's hand. Tessa could feel their pulses banging against each other in their wrists.

The four girls stared down the empty hall.

"It sounded like someone is being tortured," Sierra whispered.

"It came from the end of the hall," Tessa said.

"Well, I'm getting out of here," Brittany said, stepping back toward the elevator.

"Me too," said Sierra as she followed.

"Wait," Tessa said. She pointed down the hall. She could see someone's back, poking out of a doorway.

Eeeeeeecchhhh!

They heard the awful noise again. Only this time, Tessa realized what it was.

"It's not a person being tortured," she said, letting go of Allie's hand. "Someone's moving something. It's scraping on the floor."

They watched as a stocky young man with black hair slowly backed out of a room, holding a large wooden bed frame.

Eeeeeeecchhhh! The frame scraped the floor again and the girls heard the young man say, "Come on, Nick, try not to let it drag."

"Did he say Nick?" Brittany asked, stepping eagerly out of the elevator.

"I believe he did," Tessa replied.

Brittany turned and smiled at them. "See you girls later," she said, and started walking quickly toward the guys.

"She's unbelievable," Sierra said as they followed more slowly behind.

"She sure is," Tessa said.

"If I were her I'd be perfectly happy with Andrew," Sierra said.

Tessa stared at her. "I bet you would."

Sierra glanced at her with a surprised expression on her face, then quickly looked away. Meanwhile, Brittany had joined the two young men, who were resting the bed frame on the floor. She turned and waved for the other girls to come over.

As Tessa and the others walked down the hall, Tessa saw that the young man with Nick was stocky and well-built. From a distance Tessa thought he was as good-looking as Nick, but as she got closer she saw that his face was sort of square and he had thick, unattractive features.

He was watching Tessa, Sierra, and Allie walk toward him. Tessa had the disconcerting feeling that he was staring at her in particular.

"Sierra, Tessa, and Allie, this is Martin," Brittany said. "He works here with Nick."

"Hey, girls," Martin said. It seemed to Tessa that he was leering at her. It made her feel uncomfortable.

Brittany turned back to Nick. "When we got out of the elevator, we thought we heard a scream, and totally freaked."

"A scream?" Martin looked interested.

"It was only you guys moving the bed frame," Tessa explained.

"Yeah, it is pretty heavy," Martin said. "We've been sliding it instead of picking it up."

"At least that explains *one* of the weird sounds we've heard in this place," Sierra said.

"Oh, yeah?" Martin suddenly looked alert. "What other weird sounds have you heard?"

Nick glanced quickly at Tessa, then turned to Martin. "I think we better get this bed downstairs," he said.

"No, wait, I love hearing about the strange noises in this place," Martin said with a shark-like smile. "Anything really good?"

Suddenly Tessa decided she didn't like Martin very much.

"Well, we thought we heard loud, animal-running sounds in the attic," Sierra said. "Like a bunch of big raccoons were running around."

"In the attic?" Martin frowned and shook his head. "I was up there yesterday. There's

53

nothing up there but a bunch of junk. Maybe it was a mouse."

"But that man warned us not to go up there," Allie blurted.

"Who? You mean Sebastian?" Martin asked.

Allie nodded.

Martin grinned and shook his head. "That guy's crazy. He's still stuck in the sixties. Believe me, there's nothing in the attic to be afraid of. That is, unless you're terrified of old box springs and cabinets and stuff."

"But we did hear sounds," Brittany said. "I swear it."

Martin shrugged. "Probably from the roof, not the attic. I always hear squirrels and raccoons on the roof. But there's nothing bigger than a mouse in the attic, believe me."

"I really think we better get this thing downstairs," Nick said. He seemed impatient to get going.

Brittany must've noticed it, because she said, "You wouldn't be in a hurry to finish early tonight, would you, Nick?"

Nick seemed flustered. "Well, uh, maybe. But like I said before, I really can't tell you exactly what time I'll get off work."

"Why?" Martin said, eyeing Tessa again. "Something going on tonight? A party, maybe?"

Brittany and Tessa glanced reluctantly at each other.

"Maybe we should get together," Martin said. "I could show you all around this place. If anyone at the New Arcadia knows how to have fun, it's me."

"Well, maybe," Brittany said. Tessa noticed that her friend directed the answer to Nick more than to Martin.

"Come on, Martin," Nick said. "The front desk sent us up here twenty minutes ago. The people in 111 are waiting."

Martin smirked. "So let them wait." He grinned at the girls. "These people break their bed and then they get mad because it takes us half an hour to replace it."

Nick and Martin lifted the bed frame up and started carrying it down the hall.

"Don't forget," Brittany called after Nick. "If you do finish early, we'll be here."

"You mean, *you'll* be here," Sierra corrected her. "I'm not sure the rest of us want to get involved with those guys."

"I guess there's someone else *you'd* rather be involved with," Brittany snapped back.

Tessa was getting really tired of their bickering. "Look, let's just go into the room, okay?"

"Isn't there anyplace else to go?" Brittany asked. "Like a club or a disco or something? I mean, I really didn't come here expecting to go back to my room to go to sleep right after dinner."

"Well, I don't know about you guys, but I'm kind of worn out," Tessa said. "After getting stuck in that stairway I'm not so sure I want to party tonight. I wouldn't mind going back to the room . . . at least for a while." She glanced curiously at Allie, who nodded as if she agreed.

"Oh, okay," Brittany said, making it clear that she'd go but that she wasn't happy about it.

Back in the room, Brittany slipped on some earphones and started listening to a CD on her portable disk player. Sierra turned on the TV. Tessa decided to take a shower. She slowly pushed open the bathroom door and carefully looked around for spiders. Seeing none, she slipped out of her clothes and into the shower.

The hot water soothed her ragged nerves. It had been a strange day. First that long bus ride to the middle of nowhere, then following Sebastian to the inn, then hearing the strange noises and being trapped in the stairwell. Maybe that hadn't been as serious as it had seemed at the time, but for a few moments Tessa had been almost certain that she would die if she lost her grip on the rail. And overshadowing the whole day was the tension be-tween Sierra and Brittany. Altogether, it had been a tiring experience. Not at all what she'd expected from a weekend in the country. Some vacation it was turning out to be!

Tessa finished her shower and dried off. Then she put on her robe and blew dry her hair. Moments later she stepped back into the room. Sierra was glued to the TV. Brittany was lying on her bed with her eyes closed, her only sign of life being one finger tapping in time to the music coming through her headphones. Tessa looked around. There was no sign of Allie.

"Does anyone know where Allie went?" she asked.

Neither Brittany nor Sierra responded.

"I said," Tessa repeated in a louder voice, "does anyone know where Allie went?"

This time Brittany opened her eyes and Sierra looked up from the TV.

"She isn't here?" Sierra asked, surprised.

"Did you see where she went?" Tessa asked.

"Maybe she's in the bathroom," Brittany said with a shrug.

"No, I was just in the bathroom," Tessa said. "I can't believe she left and you guys didn't even notice."

"Chill out," Sierra said. "We're not her baby-sitters."

"Maybe not, but you could at least treat her like she's a human being," Tessa said irritably.

"A very strange human being," Brittany said.

"No stranger than you, Brittany," Tessa snapped.

"What's bugging you?" Sierra asked.

Tessa realized her friend was right. She was acting pretty irritable. Maybe it was because she'd hoped that after her shower she could relax awhile. Instead she came out of the bathroom to discover that Allie had disappeared. Well, it wasn't really her friends' fault. Tessa crossed the room to the door and pushed it open.

Allie was standing in the middle of the hall, staring up at the ceiling. She was wearing a nightgown and a robe.

"Allie," Tessa said, "what are you doing?"

"Shhh." Allie put her finger to her lips. "Listen."

Tessa listened, but didn't hear anything.

"For what?" she asked.

"I thought I heard it," Allie said.

Chapter 7

Tessa felt a chill run through her. She stared up at the ceiling and waited. She still didn't hear anything, but the thought of something up there made her heart beat fast and her blood run cold.

"Tessa?" Brittany and Sierra came out into the hall behind her and stopped.

"Is there any particular reason why the two of you are standing out here in your pajamas, staring at the ceiling?" Brittany asked.

"Allie thought she heard something," Tessa said.

"Oh, really?" Brittany rolled her eyes in obvious disbelief. "Something new?"

"That Martin guy said there was nothing up there," Sierra said.

"He could have been wrong," Allie suggested.

"I think he'd know better than you," Brittany replied. "After all, he works here."

"Well, so what's the big deal?" Sierra asked. "We know it has to be a raccoon or something."

"If it's the same thing I heard before, it doesn't sound like a raccoon," Tessa said.

"Oh? And I suppose you know what a raccoon sounds like," Brittany said.

"Not exactly," Tessa said. "But I can *imagine* what it sounds like, and that wasn't it."

"Wait a minute," Sierra said. "You're arguing about a sound you haven't even heard. I mean, not since a couple of hours ago."

Allie stepped to the wall and rapped on it with her hand. "Now what?" Brittany asked. "Don't tell me you think it's going to knock back? Are we going to *communicate* with the thing in the attic?"

They waited, but there was no response.

"There's nothing up there," Brittany said firmly.

Tessa turned to Allie. "Do you really think you heard the scampering again?"

Allie nodded.

Brittany rolled her eyes again. "Look, I'm going back in the room. If you guys want to spend the rest of the night staring at the ceiling, it's fine with me, but I have better things to do."

"Like what?" Sierra asked, as she started to follow Brittany inside.

Tessa glanced at Allie, who still hadn't moved.

"You coming?" Tessa asked.

"No," Allie replied. "I'm going up to the attic."

The other three girls stopped and stared at her.

"I don't think I heard you correctly," Brittany said.

"Yes, you did," said Sierra. "She wants to go up to the attic."

"Why?" Tessa asked.

"Because I thought I heard that noise again," Allie said. "I'm curious."

"Well, just because you *thought* you heard something doesn't mean you have to go up and look for it," Brittany said.

"But I want to," Allie said.

Brittany shook her head and turned to Tessa. "You deal with her," she said. "I'm going back into the room."

"Just remember," Sierra said. "Curiosity killed the cat."

Tessa watched as Brittany and Sierra went back into the room.

"Want us to close the door or leave it open for you?" Sierra asked.

"Close it," Tessa said.

61

Tessa waited until Sierra had shut the door, then turned to Allie. "Please don't go up there," she said.

"Why not?" Allie asked.

"Because Sebastian told us not to," Tessa said.

"But Martin said Sebastian was out of it," Allie said. "He said there's nothing up there."

"But *you* heard something," Tessa asked.

Allie shrugged slightly. "I thought I did. That's why I want to go up. I want to make sure I'm not imagining things."

"What's the difference whether you are or you aren't?" Tessa asked.

"Wouldn't it bother you if you didn't know?" Allie asked back.

Tessa sighed. She didn't know, and it didn't bother her. The thing that bothered her was how all this was making Allie appear stranger and stranger to her friends. "Look, Allie, I really don't care whether you go up there or not. It's just that . . . Well, Brittany and Sierra . . ." Tessa paused. She didn't know how to say what she was thinking without insulting Allie.

"They think I'm weird," Allie said.

Inside, Tessa winced a little. It must be very hard for Allie to hang around Sierra and Brittany, knowing how they felt about her.

"I'm worried that if you go up there they're

going to think you're even weirder," Tessa said.

"Maybe I don't care what they think," Allie said.

Tessa couldn't help smiling. *Good for you,* she thought. Maybe she was wrong about Allie. Maybe she was stronger inside than she appeared to be outside. Meanwhile, Allie started down the hall toward the stairway closest to their room. Tessa suddenly had a thought.

"Uh, Allie?"

Allie stopped and looked at her. "Yeah?"

"You're going now?" Tessa asked.

"Sure, why not?"

Tessa let out a big sigh. There was no way to stop her, and yet Tessa felt responsible for what happened. "Wait a sec, okay? Let me tell Sierra and Brittany I'm going with you."

"You don't have to," Allie said.

"I know," Tessa said. "But I want to."

She pushed open the door to their room and stuck her head in. Brittany and Sierra were sitting on their beds. The TV was off, and Brittany wasn't listening to her CD. To Tessa it was obvious they were waiting for her.

"Where's Indiana Jones?" Brittany asked.

"She wants to go to the attic," Tessa said.

"Good for her," Brittany said.

"I'm going with her," Tessa said.

Her friends looked at her with shocked expressions.

"Did she beg you?" Brittany asked.

"No. I just can't let her go up there alone," Tessa explained.

"Why not?" Sierra asked.

Tessa let her hands flop helplessly to her sides. "I don't know. Maybe because I like her." As she left the room Tessa called over her shoulder, "If we're not back in ten minutes, call the cops."

She was making a joke, but even to her it wasn't funny.

Unlike the one at the end of the hall, the stairwell nearer to their room was lit, although dimly. And it wasn't a modern design, made of concrete and steel, either. It was old and wooden with a thin oak banister. The walls were covered with peeling, yellowed flowery wallpaper. Each step creaked as Tessa followed Allie up to a closed door.

"Are you *sure* you want to do this?" Tessa asked.

"Are you scared?" Allie asked.

"In a word—yes," Tessa admitted.

Allie looked back at her and smiled. "So am I, a little. But I still can't see what the big deal is. I mean, this isn't a horror movie. There can't be a monster up there."

64

"I know," Tessa replied, but she still felt uncomfortable.

As Allie reached for the old tarnished doorknob, Tessa found herself praying it would be locked. But the knob turned and the door opened. The attic was dark, and a musty smell seeped out of it. Allie stood in the doorway and stared in. Behind her, Tessa felt her heart begin to beat hard again.

"Can you see anything?" Tessa whispered.

"A whole bunch of junk," Allie whispered back.

Tessa was still hoping Allie would lose interest and decide to turn around and go back to the room. But a moment later the blond girl stepped into the attic. Tessa let out a deep, trembling breath and followed.

The musty smell was even stronger inside the attic. The room was much larger than Tessa had imagined. She could see the vague outlines of old furniture—bedposts from a four-poster bed, overstuffed chairs, mattresses, old metal floor lamps, mirrors, and various other bric-a-brac. There were piles of box springs and other things stacked so high that it actually blocked their view. Allie had taken a few steps in and stopped. Tessa stood in the doorway.

"It looks like Martin was right," Tessa said. "Doesn't seem like there's anything up here.

At least, not anything alive."

In the dim light, Tessa saw Allie nod. "But don't you love stuff like this?" the thin girl said, running her hand over an antique framed mirror. "And look at this!" She pointed at an old, dusty bookcase. On one of the shelves was a row of antique silver candlesticks.

"Well, it is sort of interesting," Tessa said. "But I'd rather come back during the day. When there's more light."

She hoped Allie would agree and decide to return downstairs. Instead, Allie stepped farther into the attic and pointed toward the closest wall.

"I think there's a window over here," she said.

Tessa wished Allie wouldn't go any farther into the attic. Being up there in the dark gave her the creeps. Now that she was there, she almost believed the attic *was* haunted.

"Really, Allie," she said. "Why don't we come back tomorrow when it's light outside?"

"Just let me—" Allie reached toward a thin mattress propped against a wall and slid it sideways. Behind it was a window with a thin, gauzy curtain hanging over it. Suddenly the room filled with glowing moonlight. As the room brightened, Tessa looked around and saw something that made her pulse race.

"Oh no!" she gasped, lurching back toward the doorway.

"What's wrong?" Allie asked, hurrying back toward her.

"Look!" Tessa pointed a trembling finger at the bedposts for the four-poster bed. Strung between two of the posts was an enormous spider's web, the biggest one she'd ever seen. It was almost four feet across, and seemed to glow in the moonlight.

"A spiderweb," Allie said.

"You know how I feel about spiders," Tessa said. "We have to get out of here, *now*."

"I will," Allie said. "In a second."

"No, now," Tessa insisted. "I came up here with you and now I'm asking you to leave with me."

Allie stood in the moonlight. She looked almost ghostly herself. "I didn't ask you to come up here, Tessa."

She didn't say it with anger, but stated it plainly, as if she didn't understand why Tessa had followed her in the first place.

"I know you didn't," Tessa said, feeling defeated.

"Anyway," Allie said, "I promise I'll be only a minute."

To Tessa's amazement and horror, Allie stepped closer to the spider's web.

"Look how intricate and perfect it is," she

whispered. "And it's so big!"

Tessa did not share Allie's fascination. To her, a great big spiderweb meant a great big spider might be lurking about somewhere. She had no desire to be in the same room with it.

"It could never weave a web of this size outside," Allie said. "The wind would rip it to shreds. But up here, where there's no wind, the spider can weave a masterpiece."

Allie's words made Tessa feel only more uncomfortable. Maybe her friends were right, maybe Allie was a wacko.

"I have to admit I've never thought of a spider's web as a masterpiece," Tessa said nervously.

"That's understandable," Allie said. "You hate spiders. I find them fascinating. If you can forget about the spider for a moment and study its web, even you'd have to admit that it's one of nature's most beautiful creations."

"I see your point," Tessa said flatly. "I really do. But to be honest, I can't forget about that spider."

Allie glanced at her and smiled. "Okay, I won't make you stay up here any longer."

Allie stepped toward the doorway where Tessa stood waiting. They left the attic and quietly retreated to their room. When they got there, though, the door was locked.

Tessa knocked.

"Who is it?" Brittany called from inside.

"Nick," she said, trying to speak in a deep, male voice.

A moment later Brittany opened the door. "Very funny," she said dryly. Behind her, the TV was on.

"You didn't think it was Nick?" Tessa asked.

"Not for a second," Brittany said. "So, did you find anything interesting upstairs?"

Tessa and Allie glanced at each other. Tessa knew that if Allie told them about the huge spiderweb, they'd think she was weirder than ever.

"Yeah, a lot of old furniture," Allie said.

The girls came into the room. Sierra was sitting on her bed in her nightgown, brushing her long black hair.

"So, the explorers are back," she said. "Any sign of ghosts?"

"No," Tessa said. Allie went into the bathroom and shut the door.

"What about the Creature from Outer Space?" Brittany whispered.

"What about her?" Tessa replied.

"Well, what did she do up there?" Sierra asked in a low voice. "Send a message to her relatives on Mars?"

"She just looked around at the old furniture," Tessa said. "I think she's interested in antiques."

69

"I still don't understand why she wanted to go up there at night," Brittany said.

"Maybe because she's not a scaredy-cat like the rest of us," Tessa said.

"Speak for yourself, Tessa," Sierra replied.

A little while later Allie came out of the bathroom, and Tessa went in to brush her teeth. It wasn't really that late, but she felt tired after everything that had happened that day. When she came back out, Brittany and Sierra were sitting on one bed, watching TV. Allie was sitting on the other bed, reading a book.

"I don't know about the rest of you guys, but I'm pooped," Tessa said.

Brittany nodded unhappily. "Boy, I can see that this is going to be a really exciting weekend."

"Just because I'm going to bed doesn't mean the rest of you can't have fun," Tessa said.

"Oh, sure," Brittany said. "We'll have a big party."

"Who knows, maybe Nick will show up and want to go out with you," Sierra said.

"I wish." Brittany sighed.

"I'll bet you do," Sierra said.

Tessa watched as Brittany glared at Sierra.

"And I bet you'd be on the phone to Andrew telling him all about it if I did," Brittany said.

70

"Would not," Sierra snapped.

"Would too!" Brittany snapped back.

"Could we please not get into this right now?" Tessa asked wearily.

Brittany and Sierra quieted down and stared at the TV again. Tessa pulled back her side of the covers on the bed she shared with Allie. She noticed that Allie was engrossed in a Steven King book.

"Is it good?" Tessa asked.

Allie looked up from the book. "Great. I really love him. Have you ever read any of his stuff?"

"I've tried, but to tell you the truth, it gives me nightmares," Tessa admitted.

"I think he has the most amazing mind," Allie said. "I mean, I can't imagine how he thinks these things up."

Tessa yawned. She could barely keep her eyes open. "Well, good night."

"Do you want me to turn off the light?" Allie asked.

"No, it's all right," Tessa said. "If I turn away it won't bother me. But thanks for asking."

"Night, Tessa," Allie said.

Tessa slid under the covers and closed her eyes. The sheets were crisp and cool, and the pillow smelled nice and clean. In no time at all she was asleep.

Chapter 8

Tessa was alone, back in the cold, dark stairwell. She didn't know how she had gotten there. Spinning around frantically, she searched for a door to bang on, but there wasn't one. All there was were cold, gray cinder-block walls, an icy metal rail, and stairs that led nowhere.

Tessa refused to take the step into blackness. If there wasn't a door on this landing, she'd go up and find one. She started climbing the stairs. She knew she'd come to the next landing soon.

But the stairs went up and up and up. . . .

After a while Tessa had to stop climbing and catch her breath. Her legs were exhausted. She reached for the rail for support. Oddly, it had changed from metal to wood, like the banister that led to the attic. And the walls were no longer cinder block. They were covered with yellowed, flowery wallpaper.

Tessa took another breath, trying to decide what to do. Below her the steps disappeared into darkness. Above her the steps seemed to go up and up endlessly.

Then Tessa heard it—that faint, scratchy sound. It seemed to be coming from below. She didn't know what was making the noise, but she wasn't going to wait around to find out.

She started climbing the stairs again, but she wasn't getting anywhere.

The stairs had started to move. It was like trying to climb up a down escalator. . . . No matter how fast she climbed, she stayed in the same place.

And the scratching sound was growing louder.

Tessa was no longer walking up the stairs. Now she was running.

The sound grew louder still.

It didn't make sense. How could it be going up the stairs faster than she? Tessa climbed faster . . . as fast as she could. She wouldn't look behind, wouldn't look at whatever was making that noise.

The scratching noise was getting even louder.

Don't look! Don't look!

But she couldn't help it. She had to look. She turned and glanced down the stairs, but saw nothing except the rapidly receding steps disappearing into darkness.

But she could still hear the scratching noise. It sounded so close.

Tessa turned again. This time she looked at the wall.

A thin, furry leg stepped out of the shadows.

Then another.

And another . . .

Tarantulas!

Dozens of them. Big as her fist, black and furry. Crawling up the wall while she ran and ran and got nowhere on the steps.

Tessa sprinted as hard as she could, but she was losing ground now. Her heart was pounding, and she was breathing so hard her chest felt as though it might split open.

The spiders were almost upon her. . . .

No! Go away! Leave me alone!

Then she felt one on her shoulder.

"Aaaaahhhh!" she screamed, trying to knock it away. "Get off, get off!"

"Tessa!" a voice shouted. "Tessa, stop!"

A light flashed on. Tessa opened her eyes and squinted in the brightness. She felt hands on her shoulders. Allie was staring down at her. Sierra and Brittany were watching from behind Allie. Tessa's eyes darted left and right. She was in the room, in the New Arcadia.

"Spiders!" she gasped. "Tarantulas!"

"No, you were having a nightmare," Allie said. "There are no tarantulas here."

Tessa felt her body go limp. She realized she was twisted up in her sheet and blanket.

"Are you okay?" Sierra asked.

Tessa nodded. She could feel her heart still beating rapidly.

"You started kicking and thrashing in bed," Allie said. "Strange sounds were coming out of your mouth. Like you were trying to scream but it wouldn't come out. I tried to stop you because I was afraid you'd fall out of bed and hurt yourself or something."

"Thanks, but I think I'm okay now," Tessa said shakily, pushing her sheet and blanket away. She sat up on the side of her bed, aware that the others were still staring at her. Tessa looked back at them. "Really, I'm okay. I had a nightmare, that's all."

The others nodded quietly. Tessa got up and went into the bathroom, mostly to compose herself. She brushed her teeth and her hair and washed her face, then stared at herself in the mirror.

Her skin was ash white, almost as pale as Allie's.

She looked as if she'd seen a ghost.

When Tessa left the bathroom, she found that all the lights in the bedroom were on, and her friends were sitting on their beds, dressed in their pajamas, but wide awake.

"What's going on?" she asked.

Brittany looked at the others, and then back at Tessa. "I don't think anyone feels like sleeping."

Sierra and Allie nodded in agreement. Tessa realized that even she felt wide awake.

"Well, you wanted to stay up late," Tessa said to Brittany. "I guess you got your wish."

"What can we do?" Sierra asked.

"Watch TV?" Tessa asked.

"There are only a lot of weird talk shows and bad movies on at this time of night," Sierra said. "There's really nothing good on."

"What about MTV?" Brittany asked.

"Nah. I'm not in the mood," Sierra said.

"How about cards?" Brittany asked, reaching into her bag and pulling out a pack. "Anyone up for hearts?"

"I, uh, don't know how to play any card games," Allie said.

"Why am I not surprised?" Brittany asked with a sigh.

"There's no reason to act like that," Tessa said. "There are lots of people who don't know how to play hearts."

"Well, excuuuse me," Brittany replied.

"Why don't *you* come up with something to do, Tessa? After all, it's thanks to you that we're all so wide awake."

"Okay, I will," Tessa said, and thought for a moment. Then she smiled. "I know the perfect game for a late night in an inn in the woods."

"Let me guess," Brittany said snidely. "Charades?"

"Oh, I love charades!" Allie gasped.

Brittany rolled her eyes.

"No," Tessa said with a grin. "Let's play truth or dare."

Tessa wasn't surprised that Sierra and Brittany immediately stared at each other.

"What a great idea!" Brittany said with a wicked smile.

"No." Sierra shook her head. "I don't feel like it."

"Something wrong?" Brittany asked.

"No. I just don't feel like it," Sierra replied crossly.

"Oh, come on," Tessa said. She hoped that if the truth about Andrew finally came out, Sierra and Brittany might somehow deal with it instead of sniping at each other all weekend.

"I bet Allie would love to play, wouldn't you?" Brittany asked, turning to the thin girl.

"Actually, I've never played that, either," Allie admitted.

"Never played truth or dare?" Brittany's jaw dropped. "Then we *have* to play it!"

"Maybe I'll watch television after all," Sierra said.

"Chicken," said Brittany.

Sierra glared at her. "I am not."

"Then play," Brittany said.

Sierra stared at her for a long time. "Okay," she said finally, "I will."

The girls sat cross-legged in a circle on one of the beds. Brittany faced Sierra while Tessa explained the game to Allie.

"Here's how the game works," Tessa said. "One of us will say truth or dare to you, and you have to choose. If you choose truth, you have to answer truthfully any question the person asks. If you choose dare, you have to do whatever the person dares you to do."

"Can't I choose truth and then lie?" Allie asked.

"You really have to tell the truth," Sierra said. "Otherwise the game is meaningless."

"But how would you know?" Allie asked. "I mean, none of you know me."

"We wouldn't," Brittany said. "But *you'd* know you lied, and you'd have to live with that guilt forever."

"Give me a break," Tessa said, shaking her

79

head. She turned to Allie. "You're really supposed to tell the truth."

"We also have a rule that the person who suggests the game gets asked the first question," Sierra said. "Which means Tessa gets to go first."

"How does the game end?" Allie asked.

"Anyone can decide to end it," Sierra said. "But only after everyone's taken the same number of turns."

"Okay, let's start," Tessa said. "Who's going to ask me?"

"I will," said Sierra.

"Shoot," Tessa said. She was already feeling the nervousness that made the game exciting.

"Truth or dare?" Sierra asked.

Tessa puzzled over all the questions Sierra might be able to ask. The touchiest one would involve Sierra and Andrew, but Tessa knew Sierra would never bring that up.

"Truth," Tessa said.

"Okay," Sierra said with a malicious grin. "Tell us what you really, truly think of Allie."

Tessa felt relieved. "I can honestly say that I like Allie, even though I do think she's kind of different."

Sierra and Brittany looked disappointed. Allie smiled. Then Brittany got a devilish look in her eyes.

"Okay, Allie," she said, "truth or dare?"

80

Allie thought for a moment and then said, "Truth."

"What do you think of Sierra and me?" Brittany asked.

"I think you're both a little stuck-up and mean," Allie replied calmly. "But I also think you'd each be nicer if you weren't with your friends."

"A politician," Brittany muttered.

"My turn," Allie said. "Brittany, truth or dare."

Brittany looked back at her and smiled. "Truth."

"Okay," Allie said. "If you had to kill one person in this room, who would you pick?"

Brittany looked surprised. Even Tessa was a little shocked. Allie's question was both blunt and brutal, which of course made it perfect for truth or dare. Since she was a beginner at the game, though, the other girls were a bit stunned that Allie had come up with it.

Brittany's eyes shifted from Tessa to Allie and back. Finally her gaze leveled on Sierra. "I guess I'd kill you, Sierra," she said.

The room was quiet for a moment. Tessa knew that Brittany really meant it. Sierra stared at Brittany with a shocked and angry look on her face. Finally Tessa cleared her throat.

"It's Sierra's turn," she said.

"No," Brittany said. "I want to go. Truth or dare, Sierra."

Tessa felt goose bumps run up her arms. She was sure Brittany was going to ask something about Andrew. That was why Sierra hadn't wanted to play the game in the first place. Sierra's head had drooped toward the floor.

"This is a stupid game," she muttered into her chest.

Even Tessa was starting to think that she'd made a mistake by suggesting it. Instead of helping to work things out between Brittany and Sierra, it might only make things worse.

"I think Sierra's right," Tessa said. "Maybe we shouldn't do this."

"Everybody else has gone," Brittany said. "You know the rules. It can't end until everyone's gone an equal number of times. Sierra's the only one left."

"I don't mind stopping," Allie said.

"Can't we break the rules this once?" Tessa asked.

"No," Brittany said, still staring at Sierra. "What's it going to be, Sierra? Truth or dare?"

Tessa watched Sierra gaze uncomfortably at the floor. She understood the dilemma Sierra faced. She could either say truth and have to answer the inevitable question about Andrew, or she could say dare. But if she said dare, she would have to do whatever Brittany told her to do. And it was becoming obvious that Brittany would be vicious.

Brittany turned to Allie. "By the way, there's one more rule. Sometimes people think they can get out of the game by simply not saying truth or dare. So we have a rule that you have one minute to decide. If you haven't decided by then, the person who asked gets to choose."

Brittany looked at Sierra. "Time's running out," she said. "The clock is ticking."

Sierra sighed and nodded. Her lips moved and Tessa heard the word "dare" uttered.

Brittany actually looked disappointed. But then a nasty smile spread across her face. "All right," she said, relishing the moment. "What shall we dare Sierra to do?"

Sierra's eyes were downcast, and Tessa knew she wasn't looking forward to whatever Brittany had in mind. Brittany took her time thinking of the perfect dare.

Finally Brittany snapped her fingers. "I've got it," she said. "Sierra has to go to the attic."

"I don't think that's fair," Tessa protested. To her, it was the worst dare imaginable.

"Fortunately, it doesn't matter what you think," Brittany replied. "She has to take the dare."

Meanwhile, Sierra hadn't moved an inch.

"Don't dawdle, dear," Brittany said nastily.

Sierra took a deep breath and glanced at the door. Tessa wondered if she'd actually do it.

Suddenly there was a knock on the door.

Chapter 9

The girls instantly frowned at each other. It was almost two in the morning. Who would be rude enough to stop by at that hour?

"Who is it?" Brittany asked.

"Uh, Nick."

Brittany smiled and got up. "Just a minute, Nick." She went into the bathroom.

"What's she doing?" Allie whispered.

"I think she's preparing to go see him," Tessa whispered back.

Brittany came back out of the bathroom. In almost no time she'd brushed her hair and applied some makeup. She grabbed a robe and opened the door.

But there was a surprise waiting for her. Not only was Nick at the door, but Martin as well.

"Uh, hi," Nick said shyly.

"Hi, Nick," Brittany said. Tessa could see that she was glad to see him, but unhappy that Martin was also there. Martin stared in at the girls.

"What is this?" he asked with a leering smile. "A pajama party?"

"Well, it *is* kind of late," Sierra replied tartly.

"See," Nick said, turning to Martin. "I told you it was too late."

"Not for me, it isn't," Martin said. It was obvious to Tessa that Martin had probably forced Nick to come up there at that hour. Now Martin stepped into the room.

"What do you say, girls?" he asked. "Feel like a party?"

Tessa stood up. She didn't like how he'd barged into the room.

"I don't think we do," she said. "It's really pretty late. We were all about to go to sleep."

"Hey, you can always sleep late tomorrow," Martin said.

"Well, we have things to do tomorrow, so we're going to go to sleep now," Tessa replied.

"Hey," Martin said, "come on, loosen up. Don't be a party pooper."

Tessa didn't like his attitude at all. "I said, we're about to go to sleep," she repeated, glaring at him.

"And *I* said I thought that was a bad idea,"

Martin replied, glaring right back.

It was becoming obvious to Tessa that she was going to have to be very firm and very direct. "Would you please leave?" she said.

"What if I said no?" Martin asked.

"Hey, come on, Martin," Nick said, reaching toward his arm.

But Martin shrugged Nick's hand off. "Stay out of this, Nick."

"You know you're not supposed to hassle the guests," Nick said.

Martin pretended to look surprised. "Who said I was hassling anyone?"

"I did," Tessa said angrily. "You're definitely hassling us."

"Well, you're a real stick-in-the-mud," Martin shot back.

"You better get out right now," Tessa said once more. "I'm going to call the front desk and complain."

Martin smiled. "Go ahead."

"I really will," Tessa threatened.

"I dare you," Martin said with a grin.

That did it. Tessa picked up the phone and dialed 0. It rang, but no one answered.

Everyone in the room was quiet while Tessa waited for someone to answer. Finally she hung up and turned to Nick.

"Isn't anyone on duty?" she asked.

Nick shrugged and nodded toward Martin.

"I am," Martin said with a triumphant smile. "Every night."

"How can you come into someone's room when you know you're not wanted?" Tessa asked.

Martin pretended to look surprised. "Not wanted?" He turned to Sierra. "Do you want me here?"

Sierra shook her head. Martin turned to Allie. "Do you want me here?"

Allie shook here head. Martin turned to Brittany. "Do *you* want me here?"

Tessa watched as Brittany glanced at Nick. Brittany and Nick held a long look and then Brittany turned back to Martin.

"No. I think Tessa's right," she said.

Martin frowned and gave Tessa an angry look. "I'll remember this," he muttered, turning toward the door.

Something about his words sent a chill through Tessa.

"Come on, Nick," he grumbled. "These boring babes really need their beauty sleep."

Nick gave Brittany a helpless look and started to follow Martin out the door.

"Uh, wait a minute!" Brittany said, and went out with them, closing the door behind her.

As soon as the door closed, Sierra and Tessa looked at each other.

"Can you believe that guy?" Sierra whispered.

"I can't believe anyone would leave him in charge of this place at night," Tessa replied.

"He was scary," Allie said.

"He was a jerk," Tessa said, agreeing.

Now the door opened and Brittany came back inside.

"What happened?" Tessa asked.

"I told Nick I'd see him in the morning," Brittany said.

"I don't believe it," Tessa said, shaking her head.

"I do," Sierra said.

"Well, I'm glad they're gone," Tessa said. "Now we can go to bed."

"No, we can't," Brittany said. "It's still truth or dare, Sierra, and I believe you chose dare."

"Can't we drop this?" Tessa asked.

"No," Brittany said.

Sierra nodded and gazed up at the ceiling as if she were staring up into the attic.

"Suppose I go with her?" Allie asked.

"That's a sweet offer," Brittany said insincerely. "But Sierra has to go alone."

"Come on, Brittany. Can't we forget about this stupid game?" Tessa said with a yawn. "Maybe if we turned off the lights we could go back to sleep."

"I think that's a wonderful idea," Brittany said. "*After* Sierra goes up to the attic."

Without a word, Sierra stood up and went to get her robe. As soon as Sierra had turned her back on the group, Tessa gave Brittany a look that said *Please don't make her do it.*

But Brittany simply smiled and shook her head.

Sierra put on her robe and walked to the door. She had a blank look on her face, but Tessa knew she hated the thought of what was coming next.

"Oh, by the way, Allie," Brittany said, "can you think of something you saw up there that Sierra could bring back?"

Allie frowned. "Why?"

"Because she wants to make sure I really go up there," Sierra answered.

"You're really adding insult to injury," Tessa said, annoyed. "Why can't you just leave her alone?"

"Because I want to *know* that she went up there," Brittany replied and turned to Allie again. "We need evidence. Can you think of anything?"

Allie thought for a moment. "Well, there were some things in an old bookcase near the door. They were like candlesticks and things."

"Perfect," Brittany said in an affected

voice. "Sierra, darling, be a dear and bring us a candlestick, will you?"

Sierra made a face at her and went toward the door. Suddenly Tessa got up. "Wait up, Sierra," she said.

"Where are you going?" Brittany asked.

"I'm going out to the hall to talk to Sierra for a second, okay?" Tessa said.

"You're not going up there, are you?" Brittany asked.

"No, Brittany," Tessa said. "I wouldn't *dare* do that."

Tessa followed Sierra out into the hall and closed the door behind her. Sierra gave her a questioning look.

"Sierra, you don't really have to go up there if you don't want to," Tessa said in a low voice. "I don't care what Brittany says."

Sierra nodded. "I appreciate it, Tessa, but it's not such a big deal. I mean, all I have to do is go up and come right down. What could happen?"

Tessa glanced up at the ceiling and back at Sierra. "Nothing, I guess. I just think Brittany's being incredibly mean."

"So what else is new?" Sierra said with a shrug.

"Well, I guess what I'm really trying to say is, instead of going up there, you could tell Brittany the truth," Tessa said.

91

Sierra stared at Tessa for a moment with surprise in her eyes. Then she stared down at the floor and shook her head. "I, uh, don't know what you're talking about."

Before Tessa could say anything more, Sierra turned and went through the door that led up the stairs to the attic.

Tessa went back into the room.

"Well?" Brittany asked.

"Did anyone ever tell you that you really are a creep?" Tessa asked.

"All the time," Brittany said with a smirk. "But as the saying goes, if you can't stand the heat . . ."

Chapter 10

The girls sat on the bed and waited for Sierra to return. No one said a word. Tessa watched the clock.

"It's been five minutes," she said.

"So?" Brittany raised her eyebrows.

"She should have been back by now," Tessa said. "The stairway is only a few doors away. It shouldn't take her this long to go up to the attic, find a candlestick, and come back down."

"Maybe Sierra hasn't even gone up yet," Brittany said. "Maybe she's standing in the hall praying we'll fall asleep or something."

Tessa got up, opened the door, and looked outside. The hallway was empty.

"She isn't in the hall," she said. "I saw her go through the door leading up to the attic."

"Then maybe she's standing in the stairway," Brittany said.

Tessa thought about going to look in the stairway, then she remembered her nightmare. She came back in and sat on the edge of the bed.

"I'm starting to get worried," she said. "There's no way it would take her this long."

"Want me to go look?" Allie asked.

"I'm telling you," Brittany said. "She's fine. She's just trying to freak us out."

"Still, it won't hurt if I go look," Allie said, getting off the bed. "And that way you'll have double proof that Sierra actually went up there."

"Okay, go ahead," Brittany said with a shrug.

Allie put her robe on. Her hand was reaching for the door when it suddenly flew open.

Sierra staggered in.

She was trembling and white as a sheet.

"What happened?" Tessa gasped.

Instead of answering, Sierra wobbled toward the chair at the desk and slumped into it.

"Sierra?" Brittany's voice was filled with sincere concern.

"Are you all right?" Allie asked.

Sierra nodded slowly. She was still trembling.

"Come on, Sierra," Brittany said. "Tell us what happened. Don't leave us hanging like this."

"I think something . . ." Sierra stammered. "I think something touched me."

"What do you mean, 'touched you'?" Brittany asked.

"Just what I said," Sierra said, shivering at the memory. "I thought I felt something touch me."

"Where?" Tessa asked.

"My leg," Sierra said.

"I think she meant where in the inn." Brittany frowned and glanced at the other girls. Tessa could see that her sympathy was starting to wear thin.

"In the attic," Sierra said.

"Did you see what it was?" Brittany asked.

Sierra shook her head.

"Where exactly were you when it happened?" Tessa asked.

"Right inside the door," Sierra said.

"And this thing touched you, but you didn't see it," Brittany said. The tone of her voice clearly indicated that she was starting to doubt Sierra's story.

"It was dark," Sierra insisted.

"And of course you didn't have time to pick up a candlestick or any other proof that you were actually *in* the attic," Brittany said.

Sierra glared at her. "I can't believe you, Brittany."

"Oh, give me a break," Brittany groaned.

"I really think there's something up there," Sierra said. "I really do. But it was dark, and by the time I looked down it was gone."

"What do you think it was?" Allie asked.

Sierra shrugged. "I don't know. An animal?"

"Did it feel cold?" Tessa asked.

"Well, no. But it wasn't hot, either."

"Was it soft or hard?" Allie asked.

Sierra thought for a moment. "Well, it was sort of soft *and* hard."

"Oh, of course," Brittany said with a smirk. "And it was also big *and* small. And round *and* flat."

"I'm serious!" Sierra said angrily.

"How could it be soft *and* hard?" Tessa asked.

"Well, at first it felt soft, but then it felt hard," Sierra tried to explain.

Brittany shook her head and sighed.

"It's true," Sierra insisted. "You have to believe me." She started to cry.

Tessa got up and put her hand on Sierra's shoulder. "It's okay," she said softly. "Really. At least you didn't get hurt."

"Oh, come on," Brittany said, disgusted. "Of course she didn't get hurt. There aren't any monsters in the attic, okay? This is just an act, Sierra's way of getting out of truth or dare."

Sierra glared at her through tear-streaked eyes. "You're such a jerk, Brittany."

"I'd rather be a jerk than a liar," Brittany shot back.

"Would you please chill out?" Tessa asked Brittany.

Allie went into the bathroom and came out with some tissues, which she gave to Sierra.

"Thanks, Allie," Sierra said with a sniff. She blew her nose and dried her tears. Tessa really didn't know whether Sierra was lying or not, and she really didn't care. As far as she was concerned, it was a stupid game and she regretted having suggested it in the first place.

"I think it's time to go to sleep," she said.

"No," Brittany said.

"Brittany . . ." Tessa began, annoyed.

"No, forget it," Brittany said. "Like I said, this is Sierra's way of getting out of the dare."

"It isn't," Sierra said.

"You say you felt something soft and hard, but you never saw it," Brittany said.

Sierra nodded. "That's right."

"How did you know you didn't just bump into a piece of furniture or something?" Brittany asked.

"Because I don't think I did," Sierra said.

"You don't *think* you did," Brittany said. "But how do you really know?"

"Because . . . because I was standing still," Sierra said.

"So? You could be standing still, and then move your leg slightly." Brittany stood up and demonstrated. Without moving her feet she bent her knee, and her leg moved.

"This isn't a trial, Brittany," Tessa said. "Drop it and let's go to bed."

"Fine," Brittany said. "But first Sierra has to tell the truth."

Sierra's head jerked up and her eyes met Brittany's.

"Can't you leave her alone?" Tessa asked.

"No," Brittany insisted. "You know the rule. Everyone has to take the same number of turns. Sierra still hasn't taken her turn."

"Well, as far as I'm concerned, she has," Tessa said.

"She didn't bring anything back from the attic to prove she went up there," Brittany said.

Tessa couldn't believe her friend. She really felt like strangling her. "I say the game is over," she said.

"I say it isn't," Brittany said. "Now, if Sierra doesn't want to take the dare, she can tell the truth."

Suddenly Sierra stood up.

"What are you doing?" Tessa asked.

"I'll go back up," Sierra said in a sad, weary

voice. "If I don't, I promise you Brittany will never let us get to sleep."

"But what about . . . ?" Tessa began.

Sierra shrugged. "I don't know. I was scared. It was dark. Maybe I did imagine it. I mean, it's just an attic, right?"

"Do you want me to come with you?" Allie asked.

"No," Brittany said. "She has to go alone. And this time don't forget to bring something back."

"I wouldn't dare," Sierra muttered. She started to go out the door.

"Wait," Tessa said. "I have an idea. Why doesn't one of us at least watch Sierra go up the stairs? That way there'll be no argument about whether she went into the attic this time."

"I'll go," Allie said, getting up.

"Does that meet with your approval?" Tessa asked Brittany.

"Fine," Brittany said with a shrug.

A moment later Allie followed Sierra out the door. As soon as they were gone, Tessa turned to Brittany. "I really don't understand you," she said angrily.

"What?" Brittany asked, trying to look innocent.

"Making her go up there again," Tessa said. "I mean, that's really cruel."

"Look," Brittany said, "it's only an attic, right? Even Sierra said so. I guarantee you she'll be back in no time with proof she was up there."

A few seconds later the door opened and Allie came back in.

"Well?" Brittany said.

"She went into the attic," Allie said.

Brittany smiled. "Believe me, this will be the fastest round trip you've ever seen."

Chapter 11

"The fastest round trip I've ever seen?" Tessa said after ten minutes had passed.

"I don't get it," Brittany replied. "I really don't."

"Well, maybe you should go up and see if Sierra's all right," Tessa said.

"No way." Brittany shook her head.

"Wow, Brittany," Tessa said. "I really love the way you insisted Sierra had to go to the attic when you're too chicken to go up there yourself."

"I am not," Brittany said.

"Yes, you are," Tessa said. "You wouldn't go up there for a million dollars."

"I would too," Brittany said.

"Then go ahead," Tessa said.

"Oh, all right." Brittany stood up and started toward the door. Suddenly she stopped.

"Look," she said, "I don't have to go up there. And neither did Sierra. It was truth or dare. If Sierra didn't want to go up there she could have told the truth."

In a strange way, Tessa knew Brittany was right. Tessa would never have tried to steal Brittany's boyfriend the way Sierra had, but if she had, she might have told the truth about it—to avoid going into the attic.

"Well, I think we should do something," Tessa said. "Sierra should have been back by now."

"Maybe," Brittany said with a smile.

"What do you mean?" Tessa asked.

"I mean, maybe this is Sierra's revenge," Brittany said. "She's mad at me for making her go up to the attic, so she's going to hide and make us worry about her."

"You have an amazing imagination," Tessa said, shaking her head.

"You don't think Sierra's capable of doing that?" Brittany asked.

Tessa yawned. "I think she'd want to come straight back here and go to bed."

"If you want, I'll go look for her," Allie volunteered.

"There you go," Brittany said with a smile.

"No," Tessa said. "I don't think it's a good idea."

"Oh, come on," Brittany said. "What's

102

wrong with letting Allie go look?"

"I think we should all go," Sierra said.

"Well, that doesn't make any sense," Brittany said. "There's no reason for all of us to go. One's enough."

Tessa couldn't help smiling. "What are you afraid of, Brittany?"

"What are *you* afraid of?" Brittany snapped back.

"I'm willing to go up there," Tessa said, although the truth was that the thought made her feel queasy. "I think we should all go together."

"Look," Brittany said irritably, "if Allie wants to go up there alone, I don't see why we should stop her."

"Because it may be dangerous," Tessa said. She was still angry at Brittany for making Sierra go up to the attic. Making Brittany come with them to go look for her seemed like a perfect way to put her in her place.

"Well, why don't we wait a few more minutes," Brittany said. "If Sierra is trying to make us worry, I'm pretty sure she'll get tired of it and come back."

Five more minutes passed. By now Tessa knew for certain that something was wrong. It was hard to imagine what the problem was, but she knew that Sierra didn't like it up there and should have returned by now.

"We have to go look for her," Tessa said, getting up.

"I really don't mind going alone," Allie said.

"Then go," Brittany told her.

"I'm going with her," Tessa said. She turned to Allie. "Come on, we'll leave Brittany here."

They started to the door, but before they reached it Brittany was on her feet.

"Wait a minute, guys," she said. "I'm coming too."

They stepped out into the empty hall. It was very late and the inn was silent. Suddenly a rumbling sound came down the hall toward them. Brittany grabbed Tessa's arm.

"What was that?" she gasped.

"Sounded like the ice machine, Brittany," Tessa said, peeling her friend's fingers off her arm.

"Oh, of course. I knew that," Brittany said with a nervous laugh.

It annoyed Tessa that Brittany was acting like such a chicken. But it didn't annoy her *that* much, mostly because inside she was feeling pretty scared too.

Allie led them to the door to the attic. In some ways she amazed Tessa. Tessa was dying to ask her why she didn't seem more concerned, but she had a feeling she already knew the answer Allie would give.

"*What's the big deal?*" she'd ask. "*It's just an attic.*"

Just an attic, Tessa told herself. What did she think was up there? Ghosts? Vampires?

Sierra was probably up there rummaging around the antiques, having totally forgotten that anyone was waiting for her.

"What are you smiling about?" Brittany asked, snapping Tessa out of her reverie.

"Oh, I was thinking that the reason Sierra hasn't come down is because she's probably going through old trunks, looking at stuff," Tessa said.

"Of course," Brittany said, obviously not believing a word of it. "Why didn't I think of that?"

Allie pulled open the door, and they all stared up at the papered walls leading to the wooden door at the top of the stairs. Tessa couldn't help recalling the nightmare she'd had earlier. She couldn't help thinking how much she would have liked to be back in the room, and how much she'd like to lock the door and crawl into bed.

Allie stepped onto the stairs. The wood creaked. Tessa followed, and Brittany went last.

"Beautiful wallpaper," Brittany quipped. "And I love the creaking stairs. Nice effect."

Allie and Tessa didn't reply.

"Wait," Brittany suddenly said behind them.

Tessa and Allie stopped. "What is it?"

"Look." Brittany pointed up at the door to the attic. "It's closed," she said.

"So?" Tessa said.

"I would have left the door open," Brittany said with a nervous chuckle.

"It might have closed accidentally," Tessa replied.

They started up the stairs again.

"Stop!" Allie suddenly whispered. The others froze behind her.

"Now what?" Brittany gasped in a hoarse whisper.

Allie turned her head and looked down at them. "Did you hear something?"

"Yeah, creaking steps," Tessa said.

"What did you hear?" Brittany asked Allie.

"I thought I heard that sound," Allie said. "You know, like scampering feet."

Brittany caught Tessa's eye. "Uh, on second thought, maybe I will stay downstairs."

"Be my guest," Tessa said.

Brittany walked a few steps down the stairs, but then stopped and looked back up at them. "What a choice," she groaned.

Allie had climbed farther toward the wooden door. Tessa followed. Out of the corner of her eye she watched Brittany on the stairs below them, trying to decide what to do.

"Oh, well, I guess I'll see what's in the attic after all," she muttered.

When Allie reached the attic door, she glanced at Tessa. Tessa expected to see a frightened or at least nervous look on the girl's face, but if anything, Allie looked wide-eyed and animated, as if she was eager to visit the attic again.

"Ready?" she asked.

Tessa nodded.

Allie reached forward and grabbed the doorknob. She turned it slowly and Tessa heard a click. A moment later the door swung open.

"Welcome to the Twilight Zone," Brittany announced behind them in a creepy voice.

Once again, a stale, musty smell wafted toward them. Instead of moving through the doorway, Allie turned and looked at Tessa. "That used to be my favorite show. Do you remember the one about—"

"Please!" Brittany gasped, interrupting her. "Please don't tell me about it."

Allie stepped into the attic, with Tessa following behind. Pale moonlight still lit the room. The furniture and other junk threw strange, angular shadows over everything. Tessa and Allie stood right inside the doorway, looking around. With the piles of furniture, trunks, and bed frames, the attic sort of resembled a shadowy maze.

"Sierra?" Tessa called.

They waited for an answer, but all they heard was silence. Tessa stared for a moment at the big spiderweb between the bedposts half a dozen yards away. She could feel her stomach start to grow tight and her mouth become dry.

"Sierra, are you up here?" she called shakily.

Again there was no answer.

"Sierra," Brittany called with an annoyed edge to her voice. "If this is some kind of game, it's really not funny. Would you please stop it and come out?"

No answer.

Tessa glanced at Brittany. "What do you think?"

"Who knows?" Brittany replied with a shrug.

Meanwhile, Allie had wandered over to the old bookcase and the row of candlesticks on it. "I don't think Sierra came up here," she said.

"Why?" Tessa asked.

"Because none of the candlesticks are missing," Allie said.

"You memorized them?" Brittany asked skeptically.

"No, but look." Allie pointed at the shelf. "If Sierra had picked one up, there'd be a spot in the dust where it had been. Even in the moonlight you'd be able to see it."

"Now she's an amateur detective," Brittany said. "A regular Nancy Drew."

"I thought you said you saw her go up here," Tessa said.

"Well, I saw her climb the stairs and start to open the door," Allie said. "But I didn't actually watch her go inside the attic."

"So you're saying maybe she came down after you left?" Brittany said.

"It's possible, I guess," Allie said.

"Good," Brittany said. "Then I think the best thing to do is look around the inn. I'll bet you anything she's downstairs somewhere, hiding and trying to scare us."

Brittany turned toward the door, but suddenly stopped and stared at it. "I'm sure I left it open," she said. The door to the stairs was now closed.

"It may have closed on its own," Tessa said.

Brittany walked to the door and grabbed the doorknob. Tessa watched as she pushed and pulled. Suddenly Brittany turned to them, her face drained of blood and her eyes wide.

"It won't open!" she gasped.

Chapter 12

Tessa felt the hair rise on the back of her neck. *This isn't happening*, she thought. *We're not trapped in the attic.*

"It won't budge," Brittany said, twisting the doorknob in vain.

"Here, let me try," Tessa said. Brittany moved away from the door. Tessa tried jiggling the doorknob, but it was useless. Next she tried to push the door, but it still wouldn't open. Finally Tessa leaned back and then hit the door hard with her shoulder.

Thunk! The door didn't move.

Thunk! She tried again.

Nothing. Tessa felt a sickening sensation in the pit of her stomach.

"Maybe if we both try," Brittany said, moving back to the door.

Together Brittany and Tessa pushed as hard

111

as they could. The door creaked under their weight, but remained shut. Finally they gave up and stared at each other in the eerie light.

"Don't tell me we're stuck up here." Brittany's voice was barely more than a terrified squeak. Tessa could feel her own heart start to pound. Her throat felt tight and it was suddenly difficult to swallow.

"We have to stay calm," she said.

"What happens if we do?" Brittany asked nervously. "We magically find a way out?"

"There has to be a way," Tessa said, her eyes darting around the attic.

"Where?" Brittany asked. "I don't see any other doors."

"We'll have to look," Tessa said. "Maybe there's one against another wall, or on the other side of the attic."

"Great," Brittany muttered. "*You* go find it. I'll wait here. Better yet, let's let Allie go looking for another door."

Allie, Tessa thought. She quickly glanced around. "Where is she?"

Tessa squinted into the dark. There was no sign of Allie anywhere.

"Didn't you see where she went?" Brittany asked.

"No."

"Great," Brittany moaned. "Allie's decided to go for a hike."

"Allie?" Tessa called.

There was no answer.

"Earth to Allie," Brittany called. "Earth to Allie."

"I'm over here," Allie called.

"Where's over here?" Brittany called. "It's too dark. We can't see."

"Around the big pile of box springs," Allie called.

Tessa felt Brittany nudge her to the right.

"You first," Brittany said.

Tessa started through the dark. She stepped carefully around the box springs. Suddenly she noticed Allie crouched on the floor, half a dozen feet away with her back to them. She wasn't moving at all. She seemed to be staring at something on the floor.

"Allie?" Tessa said.

"Yes?" Allie replied without turning around.

"What are you doing?"

"Come here and look," Allie said.

Tessa and Brittany glanced at each other and then walked toward the crouching girl. As they got near her, Allie slid around so that they could see what she was examining.

"A shoe?" Tessa frowned and squatted down for a better look. It was a white sneaker, lying on its side.

"That's Sierra's shoe!" Brittany gasped.

Tessa looked up into Brittany's terror-stricken face. "Are you sure? Was she even wearing shoes?"

"Yeah—I saw her slip them on."

"It hasn't been here long," Allie said, reaching down and touching it. "There's no dust on it."

"There's *something* on it," Tessa said. She could see some sort of film covering the shoe.

"Yes," Allie said, rubbing her fingers together. "It's sticky."

Tessa reached down and touched the shoe with her finger. A moist, sticky, silvery film came off.

"What is it?" Brittany whispered.

"I don't know," Tessa said. "It feels like cotton candy."

"Okay," Brittany said with a panicked edge to her voice. "I'm sure this is all a joke. It's Sierra's way of getting back at me. She gets us up here, she leaves her shoe with this junk on it, and she locks the door behind us . . ."

Suddenly Brittany rushed away.

"Brittany!" Tessa shouted, jumping up.

She found Brittany banging her fists against the door. "Sierra! Okay, it's very funny! Ha ha! Sierra! Can you hear me? It's time to open the door! Sierra!"

Brittany kept banging on the door and shouting, but gradually the banging stopped

114

and the shouts became sobs. She leaned against the door and slowly crumpled into a sobbing heap on the floor before it.

"Oh, please," Brittany gasped, pressing her tearstained face against the wood. "Tell me it's a joke. Please, Sierra, *please*! I promise I won't make you tell the truth. I promise. *Please!*"

The door didn't open. Tessa didn't know where Sierra was, but she doubted she was on the other side of the door, playing a trick.

"Sierra?" Brittany whimpered.

Tessa moved closer, leaned down, and put her arms around Brittany. "Come on," she said gently. "It's not that bad. The door's stuck. We're in the attic. But we'll get out."

Brittany stared at her with wide, fearful eyes. "What are you talking about? You think this is all some accident? Are you crazy? She got us up here. She locked the door behind us. You don't know her, Tessa. I do. Maybe it is a joke, maybe she is trying to scare us. But I know her. She wants Andrew. You don't know what she'd do to get him."

Actually, Tessa had an idea of what Sierra would do, but she couldn't say so. And besides, right now she was almost certain that Brittany was wrong. "What are you talking about, Brittany? I mean, even if you're right and Sierra does want Andrew, what good would it do to trap us in the attic?"

"Maybe she wants to kill me," Brittany said.

"Brittany, come on," Tessa said. "Andrew's a great guy, but believe me, no one would kill you for him."

"I think she's here," Allie suddenly said behind them. "She wouldn't leave her shoe. It's cold out. Besides, why leave only one? It doesn't make sense."

"Did anyone ever tell you that you're amazingly lame?" Brittany asked.

"Actually, Allie's probably right," Tessa said. "Why would she leave one shoe and not the other?"

"Okay, then if Sierra's here, where is she?" Brittany asked.

"Why hasn't she come out?"

"Maybe we better look for her," Tessa said.

"We could also look for another way out at the same time," Allie said.

"So we're going to stumble around in the dark looking for her?" Brittany asked.

"I have matches," Allie said.

"Oh, great," Brittany said. "Let's burn the place down. That'll be a great way to find Sierra. We'll smoke her out."

Allie reached into the old bookcase and pulled out a silver candlestick. In the moonlight Tessa could see the stub of a candle sticking out of it. Allie took a pack of matches out of her pocket and struck one. A flame burst out.

Suddenly the girls heard a loud scampering sound hurry away from them. Tessa and the others froze.

"What was *that?*" Allie said, quickly touching the match to the candle. The wick caught.

"It was that same sound," Tessa gasped.

"Then there is something up here," Brittany said. She turned toward the door, then seemed to remember that it was locked.

"I'm pretty sure it's just a raccoon or a squirrel or something," Tessa said. "We once had some squirrels in our attic."

"It's not a squirrel or a raccoon," Allie said. "It doesn't run like a four-legged animal. It doesn't *move* like a four-legged animal."

Brittany hugged herself and shivered with fear. "Great. Sierra's disappeared, and we're trapped in the attic with some weird animal. This is really my idea of a terrific weekend getaway."

"I think we should do what you said," Allie said. "Look for Sierra and a way out."

"No way," Brittany said, shaking her head. "I'm not looking for *anything* in this attic. There's something up here with us, or did you forget that already?"

"We don't have to be afraid of it," Allie said.

"How do *you* know?" Brittany asked.

"Whatever it is, it's afraid of fire," Allie said. "As long as we have the candle, we'll be okay."

Brittany blinked and looked surprised.

"She's right," Tessa said. "The second Allie lit the match it ran away."

"Boy oh boy, I really feel safe now," Brittany said.

"I think we should try to look," Tessa said. "It's better than sitting here doing nothing."

Allie turned back to the bookshelf. "Look," she said. "There are more candles." She pulled out several more candlesticks.

"Let's each take one," Tessa said.

Allie lit the other candles.

"Now, listen," Brittany said. "We're not going to split up or anything, are we?"

"No," Tessa said. "We're all staying together."

Holding her candlestick, Allie slowly started to cross the attic. Tessa and Brittany reluctantly followed.

"Hopefully there'll be another doorway or something," Tessa whispered.

Allie tiptoed through the pieces of furniture and piles of old trunks and suitcases. The attic was longer than Tessa had imagined, and so filled with junk that it was hard to see the other end. Tessa kept her fingers crossed, hoping that they'd find another door there. A door that would be open.

Suddenly Allie stopped so sharply that Tessa bumped into her.

"Wow," Allie gasped. Tessa looked over her shoulder and saw why Allie had paused. Strung across the attic before them was another spiderweb. Only, this one was even larger than the one they'd found between the bedposts. Tessa felt a cold chill run through her.

"I've never seen a spiderweb so big," Allie said wondrously.

"Well, all I can say is it must've been made by one mighty big spider," Brittany quipped.

"Brittany, please don't say that," Tessa said. She'd started to feel light-headed just at the thought of spiders. The idea of a giant one made her feel even worse.

"Well, what do we do now?" Brittany asked. "I mean, the web's completely blocking our way."

"We could go over there," Tessa said, pointing toward a shadowy area to their left.

"No," Allie suddenly said. "I really think we should go this way." Allie shrugged. "I just have a feeling."

"Oh, great," Brittany muttered. "Now we're going on her *feelings*."

"Here," Allie said. She picked up an old

curtain rod and stuck it into the web, pulling it down. "Now we can go through."

Tessa watched as Allie picked up her candlestick and started past the web.

"Go on." Brittany nudged Tessa from behind. "I don't want to get too far behind our fearless leader."

Tessa took one tentative step, then another, then three quick steps to get past the web. She realized she'd been holding her breath, and now took a deep gasp of air.

Meanwhile, Allie had stopped again ahead of her.

"Now what?" Tessa asked.

Allie didn't reply. She just pointed at the floor in front of her. As Tessa stared over her shoulder, she felt her stomach do a flip-flop.

Lying on the floor before them was a skeleton.

The skeleton of a dog.

Chapter 13

"I want to go home," Brittany whimpered, backing away.

Tessa slid her hand over Brittany's. "Don't be scared," she whispered.

"Oh, sure," Brittany replied with a frightened, brittle laugh. "I won't be scared. Like it's every day I come across a dog skeleton."

"Look," Allie said, crouching closer to the skeleton and pointing. "It's still got its collar on it."

"I really can't stand this," Brittany said.

Tessa knew she was talking about Allie's weird fascination with morbid things. She squeezed Brittany's hand. "Try to get a grip, Brit."

"Why would it still have its leash on?" Allie whispered.

"I guess that's one of the many questions

that cries out for an answer, isn't it?" Brittany asked. "Who cares if it has its leash on? What's it doing here in the first place?"

"Look," Tessa said. "Let's not worry about why it's here. It's not really important right now, is it? Someone could have put it up here as a joke. I don't know. I think we're going to scare ourselves even worse if we try to come up with an explanation."

"I don't see how I can scare myself any more than I already am," Brittany said. "First giant spiderwebs, then dog skeletons. What next?"

"I wonder if Sierra came across this," Allie said. She began to go forward. Suddenly Tessa realized Brittany wasn't behind her.

"Brittany?" she asked.

"I can't," Brittany replied in a trembling whisper.

"Why not?"

"I just can't," Brittany said. "I'm too scared. This is too bizarre. I'm going back over there and I'm going to sit and wait." She pointed toward the door they'd come in through.

"Wait for what?" Allie asked.

"Wait until morning," Brittany said. "Wait until the sun comes up and it gets lighter in here and we can see our way around. I'm tired of coming across things like dog skeletons and getting scared out of my wits."

Brittany started to walk away. Allie glanced at Tessa.

"I guess we better go with her," Tessa said. "We can't leave her alone."

They followed Brittany back to the door. Brittany went to the old bookcase and took out more candlesticks and placed them on the floor. Then she carefully lit each one from the candle she'd been carrying. Soon there were half a dozen candlesticks in a circle on the floor before her. Brittany sat down cross-legged and stared at them.

"You're welcome to join me," she said. "But you have to promise that you won't talk about scary stuff."

Tessa and Allie sat down close to the candles.

It seemed as though a long time passed. No one said anything. They just stared at the flickering flames.

"I feel like I'm at a birthday party," Tessa said, trying to lighten up the situation.

"I hope it's not our last," Brittany muttered.

"Don't say that," Tessa said. "Of course it's not."

"What about Sierra?" Brittany asked.

"We don't know what happened," Tessa said. "She could be anywhere. She might even be down in our room, wondering where in the world *we* are."

"She'd know we went up to the attic to look for her," Brittany said.

"You're going to drive yourself crazy thinking about it," Tessa said. "It's like the dog skeleton. We really don't know what happened. There's no sense in trying to speculate. We'll probably never know."

"Listen, Tessa," Brittany said. "It's the middle of the night. It's dark. I have to do something to make the time pass or I really will go crazy."

The candle flames continued to flicker. Melted wax slid down the candles and dripped onto the dusty wooden floor. Tessa tried not to think about Sierra. Every time she did, the thoughts weren't pleasant. In fact, they were horrible.

"Fire will keep the evil spirits away," Allie suddenly said.

Tessa and Brittany stared at her. The flickering candles sent strange shadows over her face.

"What?" Brittany asked.

"Evil spirits don't like fire," Allie said. "I read about it in a book."

Brittany glanced at Tessa and shook her head.

"I don't think talking about things like that is going to help us right now," Tessa said.

"Why not?" Allie asked. "It's what we're all thinking, isn't it?"

"No. I'm thinking about how to make it until morning," Brittany snapped.

Once again Allie grew quiet and seemed to withdraw.

"I'm sorry, Allie," Tessa said. "I think you're right. It's stupid to pretend that we're not afraid. I mean, Sierra's missing, the door to the attic is suddenly locked, we keep hearing those running sounds, and we saw that dog skeleton. How can you not help thinking something strange is going on?"

Allie nodded and turned to Brittany, who'd pulled her knees up under her chin.

"Well, I, for one, would like to know what it is," Brittany said.

"I don't know," Tessa said. "Maybe you really wouldn't."

The minutes passed with unbearable slowness. The girls sat in a small circle, staring at the candles. Tessa felt her eyes start to droop and fought the desire to curl up and go to sleep.

"Tessa?"

"Huh?" Tessa snapped her head up, startled.

"I think you were starting to fade," Brittany said.

"Sorry." Tessa shook her head.

"Maybe we should play twenty questions or something," Tessa said.

They started to play, but didn't get far. Nobody could keep her mind on the facts. Tessa thought Brittany's question had something to do with a famous woman scientist.

"Did you say she was dead?" Tessa asked.

"It's a *he*, Tessa," Brittany corrected her. "And yes, he's dead."

But Tessa wasn't listening. She was watching Allie, whose eyelids had closed. The thin girl's head tipped forward.

"Should we wake her?" Brittany asked.

"I don't think so," Tessa said. "She'll probably only fall asleep again."

"Okay, but let's not let each other fall asleep."

"Definitely," Tessa said.

The candles were burning low. One by one, Tessa watched them sputter and go out, leaving a thin wisp of light gray smoke curling slowly upward.

What would happen when the last candle went out?

Tessa sat and watched the last candle's flame grow smaller and flicker as if it were desperately gasping for breath.

Then, finally, it too went out.

The attic was plunged into darkness. Tessa sat motionless, listening for the sound . . . for any sound . . .

And then she heard it. The faintest sound of scratching.

Tessa stared into the dark, but she could see nothing.

The scratching grew louder. . . . It seemed to be coming from all around her.

Tessa's eyes darted left and right, but she could see nothing but blackness. Were they out there? The tarantulas? Were they making that scratching sound? Were they coming closer?

Tessa's eyes burst open. For a moment she didn't know where she was. It was dark, and a slightly acrid, smoky smell hung in the air. Then the realization of where she was came back. She was in the attic, with Allie and Brittany.

But it shouldn't have been dark.

What happened to the candles?

Tessa looked to her right . . . and saw nothing. Where was Brittany? She'd been sitting on Tessa's right . . . She quickly turned to her left. In the dim moonlight she saw Allie with her knees pulled up under her chin. Her arms were wrapped tightly around her legs, and she stared back at Tessa with eyes nearly as wide as saucers. The girl looked even paler than normal, but that might have been because of the dim light.

"Where's Brittany?" Tessa asked.

Allie stared back at her and didn't answer. She had a strange, hopeless look on her face.

127

"Allie?"

Still no answer. Suddenly Tessa realized that the girl hadn't moved or blinked. She seemed to be in a trance. Tessa gently shook her shoulder.

"Allie, are you okay?"

Allie blinked, but still said nothing.

"What is it?" Tessa asked, feeling the hair on the back of her neck start to rise. "Where's Brittany?"

Allie's lips started to move. "I saw it," she whispered.

"Saw what?" Tessa asked, feeling a chill. "You saw something? What was it?"

Allie turned and stared off into the shadows. Tessa looked also. Allie was saying there was something in the shadows. Was it the thing that made the scampering sound? Tessa felt her stomach tighten nervously.

It was afraid of fire. . . .

Tessa stared down at the candlesticks. She could barely make out the curved shape of several wicks sticking out of candle stubs. If there were still candles, why weren't they burning?

"Where are the matches?" Tessa quickly asked.

Allie didn't respond. Tessa didn't have time to fool around. She reached toward the pocket of Allie's robe where she'd seen her put the matches. She gently slid the pack out and quickly lit one.

The stub of a candle lit. Tessa frowned. She had expected to find that the candles had burned out. Obviously they hadn't. Had someone blown them out? Why?

Tessa quickly lit the rest of the candles. If there really *was* something out there, and it was afraid of the fire, she wanted to keep it away.

If Allie noticed Tessa light the candles, she made no indication of it. Tessa reached toward the blond girl again. This time she shook her harder. "Allie!"

Allie's head wobbled on her shoulders as if it was only loosely connected.

"What's wrong with you?" Tessa asked, her stomach churning. She practically had to hold Allie's head and turn it toward her. "What happened? Where's Brittany?"

"She's gone," Allie said.

"Where? Did you see her go?"

Allie began to nod, then changed and shook her head.

"Is that a yes or a no?" Tessa asked.

"I saw her, but I didn't," Allie said.

Tessa felt ready to scream, or slap Allie. Instead she tried to get control of herself.

"Now, listen, Allie," she said, trying to stay calm. "This is important. This is *serious*. You have to tell me what you saw. You have to tell me what happened to Brittany."

"It took her away," Allie said.

"What took her away?"

"I don't know."

"You know something took Brittany away, but you don't know what it was?"

Allie nodded.

"Well, what did it look like?" Tessa asked.

"It looked . . ." Allie faltered. "It looked dark. I couldn't really see it."

"But you're sure there was something," Tessa said. "And it took Brittany away?"

Allie nodded.

Tessa leaned closer to Allie. "Allie, this is important. Did you *really* see it take Brittany away? I mean, is it possible you dreamed it or something?"

Allie responded by slowly waving her arm around. "Do you see her?"

Tessa sighed. Allie had a good point.

"Okay, but there's something I don't understand," Tessa said. "Why were the candles out? If something took Brittany away, why didn't we hear it?"

"I did," Allie replied.

"If you heard it, how come you didn't see it?" Tessa asked. "What happened to the candles?"

"I don't know."

They were getting nowhere. And Brittany was gone. Sierra was gone. Something incredibly strange and scary was going on.

"Allie, we have to get out of here," Tessa said, getting up.

Allie didn't move from the floor. She didn't even look up. Tessa felt terrified and weary.

"Allie, please, *please* get up."

If Allie heard her, she made no sign of it. Tessa sighed. Maybe she didn't have to get Allie up. It was more important to find a way out right now. If she found one, *then* she could get Allie to move.

But how would she get out? She knew the door was locked. Maybe she could find something to break it down with. Tessa looked around and then back at Allie. Could she leave her there? Hopefully, she wouldn't have to go far to find something to break the door with.

"Allie," Tessa said.

The girl didn't move. Tessa kneeled down and faced her. Maybe this was how Allie dealt with fear. Maybe she was totally falling apart inside. Tessa ran her fingers through Allie's long, wispy hair. Allie blinked and looked up at her.

"I'm going to go look for something to break the door down with," Tessa said gently.

131

"I hope I won't have to go far. You don't have to come with me if you don't want to. You can just stay here."

Allie blinked again. Tessa took that as a "yes." She slid the remaining candlesticks closer to Allie, so the flames were as close to the girl as possible. Then Tessa stood up, taking one candle for herself.

"I'll be right back," she said.

Allie still didn't reply, but Tessa thought she understood. She turned to look around. The attic was dark and cluttered. Tessa tried to remember if she'd seen anything earlier that might work as a battering ram. She stepped around an old chair and held the candle out. Ahead of her was a table lying on its side. To her right were some old paintings in frames. To her left was that bed frame, the one with the spider's web between the posts.

Bedposts . . .

Maybe she could use one. If she could get it free from the frame, maybe she could use it to break down the door.

But the spider's web was attached to it. . . .

She couldn't worry about that now. Tessa took a deep breath and walked toward it.

Ahead of her, the spider's web glowed faintly in the moonlight like an intricate, silvery fishnet. Tessa took another step. She'd have to use something to knock the spider's web off the post. She looked around and saw something lying on the floor. She looked closer. It was a shoe. Just like the one they'd found before. It was Sierra's other shoe.

Tessa felt her throat tighten. Her heart was beating so loud she could feel it in her ears. To her, finding one shoe had still left open the possibility that Sierra was playing some kind of game with them, that she'd left it up there on purpose to make them wonder and worry.

But two shoes . . .

Tessa kneeled down and reached out toward the sneaker. Like the other, it was covered with a moist, sticky substance. Suddenly Tessa saw something lying a few feet in back of the shoe. Something dark and large. It looked like a bundle or a sack, but it had a human shape. Her heart thumping in her throat, Tessa looked closer.

It *was* a human shape, wrapped in a silken cocoon.

Clank!

The candlestick fell out of Tessa's hand and clattered to the floor.

It was Sierra.

Chapter 14

Tessa put her hand over her mouth and stifled the scream that was rising out of her lungs. Her legs felt weak, and she grabbed a nearby chair to steady herself. She could taste bile in her throat. The candle had gone out when it hit the floor, but in the pale moonlight Tessa could see her friend through the gauzy silken cocoon. Sierra's skin was gray, her cheeks were hollow, and her eyes were sunken. She looked unnaturally emaciated.

Tessa stared at her for several long moments, hoping to see some movement, praying Sierra's chest would expand and contract with a breath. But Sierra was still.

Tessa felt her heart sink.

Sierra was dead.

Tessa backed away. She didn't want to think about how her friend had been killed or why she was in that cocoon. She just wanted to get out of the' attic. In her growing panic, though, she couldn't remember the way back to Allie.

"Allie?" she called loudly. Staring around the attic, her view was blocked by the furniture and junk that was piled almost up to the ceiling in some places.

"Allie!"

There was no answer. Maybe Allie was just being mute—still in her trance. Or maybe the thing that had gotten Sierra had also gotten her.

"Allie!" she shouted. "Please answer me!"

There was no reply. Tessa stared around in the eerie dimness. She took a few steps to the left. The bedposts and spiderweb came into view. No, she wasn't going that way, not now.

She turned to the right and passed an old bureau. It didn't look familiar, but maybe she'd passed it before without noticing. After all, everything looked different without candlelight. Tessa came around the bureau and suddenly stopped.

She thought she heard something.

Tessa held her breath. Was it the scampering sound she'd heard? From somewhere in the dark came soft rapid thuds. . . .

There it was again. Was it close to her? Was it after her?

Tessa spun around and took a step.

Oooofff! She tripped over something and fell, banging her knees and hands on the hard wooden floor.

She quickly turned around to see what she'd tripped over.

There, lying on the floor, with open, unblinking eyes, was Brittany.

"*Brittany!*" Tessa screamed, crawling across the floor to her friend. "*Brittany, are you okay?*"

She reached the girl and grabbed her shoulders, pulling her up slightly. Brittany's head flopped back. Her eyes remained open. Now Tessa saw the small trail of blood leaking from the corner of Brittany's mouth.

Brittany was dead, but she still felt warm.

Tessa jumped up. Where was it? Was it hiding from her? Tessa's heart was beating like a jackhammer. Her skin felt hot and tight. Her mouth was dry, and a nauseated sensation filled her stomach.

Suddenly she saw a flicker of light and shadow against an old chair covered with a dusty white sheet.

Allie!

Tessa rushed toward the flickering light. Had it gotten her, too?

No . . .

Tessa followed the light and found Allie

137

sitting where she'd left her in front of the few remaining flickering candles. She quickly crouched down before the dazed girl.

"We have to get out of here, Allie," she said loudly. "You have to snap out of this daze. Sierra and Brittany are dead. Whatever you saw got them. Now we have to go!"

Allie stared into the air between them, her eyes unfocused.

"Stop it, Allie!" Tessa screamed.

The girl didn't respond.

Smack! Tessa slapped her across the cheek. Allie turned her face away and looked down at the ground. Tessa stared at her in disbelief.

"You've given up, haven't you?" Tessa gasped. "You just don't care."

Allie didn't reply. Tessa turned back to the bookcase. There was one old candlestick left, with just the nub of a candle in it. Tessa grabbed it and lit it off the candle on the floor in front of Allie.

"I'm going to find a way out of here," she said. "And when I do I'm going to come back and get you."

Allie showed no sign of hearing her.

Tessa stared at her and shook her head. "I'll be back," she said, and turned away into the darkness.

Holding the candle before her, she made her way back into the attic. She knew the

138

thing that had killed Sierra and Brittany was out there somewhere, but she also knew that it didn't like fire. She told herself that as long as she had the candle she'd be okay.

She almost believed it.

Tessa stepped carefully around each chair and couch, looking up and down and in every direction. It was a long attic, and they'd explored only one side of it. There might be something on the other side, some way out.

Tessa weaved in and out of piles of old box springs, more trunks, and even an old canoe. As she'd walked toward the center of the attic it had grown darker, but now it began to get lighter again. Ahead, she caught glimpses of another window letting in the moonlight. Tessa headed toward it. Maybe it opened onto a roof. Maybe they could break through it and climb down.

She got to the window and looked out. The full moon was high in the sky, surrounded by twinkling stars. Oh, how she wished she were out there somewhere. But she looked down and her hopes instantly disappeared. There was a straight drop three stories down.

Tessa turned around and looked back into the dark attic. Somewhere in there was the thing that killed Sierra and Brittany. And Allie was in there too. Tessa's terrified heart broke for her. The poor girl was obviously scared out of her mind. Tessa knew that if she didn't get them out of there soon, she and Allie would die as well.

Tessa began thinking about the door again. If only she could find something to break it down with. She hunted around some more. In the corner she saw what looked like a small, metal end table. Maybe she could try banging it against the door.

Tessa stepped toward the table, then said, "Ow!" as she stubbed her toe on something on the floor. Looking down, she realized she was staring at some kind of metal latch. Tessa held the candle closer to the floor. Now she could see the outline of a square cut into the floor. On the opposite side of the square from the latch was a pair of hinges!

Tessa couldn't believe what she'd stumbled upon. She dropped to her knees, grabbed the latch, and pulled. A trapdoor! What incredible luck! Tessa pulled the trapdoor up. Below was the maroon-carpeted hallway. Tessa stared at it, almost delirious with relief. All she had to do was drop through it and she was saved!

Allie.

Tessa glanced across the dark attic. There was no doubt in her mind about what would happen if she left Allie, even if it was just long enough to get help. Allie was helpless and defenseless. It was true that she hadn't responded to anything Tessa had said, but surely news of a way to safety would snap her out of her daze.

Tessa looked down into the hall once more. Safety was right there, only a few feet away. . . .

She was so tempted to drop through the trapdoor. But Allie had been the one who'd reached out for her in the stairwell. She'd saved Tessa's life.

Tessa couldn't leave her. She knew she'd never be able to live with herself if she did.

Still holding her candle, Tessa made her way back across the attic. She was careful to memorize the way back to the trapdoor. Each time she came around another pile of junk, she expected to see the flickering light from Allie's candle, but it wasn't there.

Finally Tessa knew she'd crossed almost the entire attic. A new sense of dread began to grow inside her. Where was Allie? Why hadn't she seen the flickering light and shadows from her candle?

Tessa began to search for her. She'd begun to fear the worst. *No, please*, she prayed. *Don't let it happen to Allie, too.*

Suddenly her foot hit something. Tessa looked down and saw candlesticks lying at her feet. When she looked up she saw something that made the blood drain out of her.

Half a dozen feet away, Allie lay on the ground, half covered by a huge, black furry thing.

Tessa froze. As she watched, the furry thing began weaving the same silken cocoon around Allie that Tessa had found Sierra wrapped in.

Now Tessa knew what it was.

It was huge and had eight legs, each perhaps two feet long.

It was a spider, a huge, giant, tremendous spider.

Chapter 15

Tessa was running, stumbling, crashing into things. She only had one thought in her mind—she had to get to the trapdoor. She had to get out. Nothing else mattered. . . .

Somewhere along the way she dropped her candle, but she didn't care. Some extreme sense of urgency and survival guided her to the place where the trapdoor was.

Half a dozen feet from the trapdoor, Tessa suddenly froze. There was someone there! Someone had stuck his head through the trapdoor! The person was facing away from her, looking around.

Tessa took another step, and the person turned toward her. It was Martin! For a second they stared at each other.

"So, it's you," Martin said with a chuckle.

"I'm trapped up here," Tessa gasped.

"There's a huge spider. It's killed my friends."

Martin curled his lower lip. "Aw, boo hoo. Isn't that sad."

"I'm serious," Tessa said, her voice cracking.

"I bet you are," Martin said.

"It's back there somewhere," Tessa said, pointing into the dark. "I saw it. If I don't get out of here soon it's going to get me, too."

"You really think so?" Martin asked.

Tessa couldn't believe how he was toying with her. "Let me come down," she said.

"Why should I?" Martin asked.

"You wouldn't leave me up here," Tessa said desperately. "It'll kill me. Don't you understand?"

"Oh, yeah, I understand," he said. The next thing Tessa knew, Martin reached over and started pulling the trapdoor closed.

"You . . . you can't do this," Tessa cried. "You're going to leave me to be killed!"

"Tsk, tsk," Martin said, shaking his head. "What a waste."

"This is a joke, right?" Tessa said quickly. "You're trying to teach me a lesson because I was rude to you tonight, right?"

Martin stopped pulling the trapdoor down for a moment. "Teach you a lesson? No, I want to do *more* than teach you a lesson."

"Please," Tessa gasped. "*I'll do anything!*"

"Too late."

Bang! The trapdoor slammed shut. Tessa dropped to her knees and yanked on the latch. It wouldn't open.

"Martin!" she screamed. "Martin, please! You can't do this! It'll kill me!"

But the trapdoor didn't budge.

Oh, no! Oh, please, no! Tessa yanked desperately on the latch. It *had* to open! Martin had to let her down. No one could be *that* cruel! *That* sick!

Tessa felt tears fall from her eyes. She pulled and pulled until her hands hurt.

It was useless. Like the attic door, the trapdoor was now locked. And she was trapped in the attic. Martin wanted her to die.

Exhausted, panic-stricken, and hopeless, Tessa kneeled on the floor next to the trapdoor and cried. It was so incredibly unfair. . . . She'd never done anything to deserve this. *Never!*

Why did she have to come to the New Arcadia?

Why did it have to kill her friends?

Why didn't it just leave her alone?

Why? *Why?*

Tessa didn't know how long she stayed like that on the floor of the attic, but after a while, some sixth sense told her to look up.

On the floor, a dozen feet away, crouched the spider.

Tessa stood up slowly and backed toward the window.

The spider didn't move.

Tessa had to assume it would come after her. It had gone after her friends.

Storing up for winter . . .

The memory of Allie's words sent shivers of fear and revulsion through her. Imagine being wound up in a cocoon, being stored for dinner on some cold and wintry night. . . .

Tessa couldn't take her eyes off the huge spider. But the creature didn't move. What was it waiting for?

Tessa stood and watched it in terror. Her breaths were short and quick. Despite the cool air, a light perspiration dotted her forehead. Her hands shook. She didn't dare leave the window. Any step away from it would be toward that horrible monster.

Why didn't it do anything? Either go away or come closer—Tessa almost didn't care. But she couldn't stand just waiting there.

The spider remained motionless, as if it was sizing her up. Tessa desperately thought back to school biology. With a shiver she remembered the diagram of a spider she'd seen in one of her textbooks. How many eyes did it have? Six? Eight? She couldn't recall now.

146

All she could remember was how horribly ugly it was. How horribly ugly those eyes were.

"What are you waiting for?" she heard herself say. "Is this a game? Are you trying to torture me? I hate you. You hear me? I hate you!"

The spider just stood there, waiting.

Tessa couldn't stand it anymore. Someone had left an empty soda bottle on the windowsill. She picked it up and threw it at the spider.

Clunk! It thudded on the ground, making the creature jump a foot to its right.

Tessa shook her head wearily. She had never had good aim.

Once again the spider settled down to wait. Tessa wondered if she could sprint past it. But if she did, where would she go? Where *could* she go to get away from it?

Nowhere. She was trapped in the attic. There was no place to go.

Tessa didn't know what to do. She couldn't give up and she couldn't fight it. She wished it would *do* something.

And then suddenly Tessa got her wish.

It moved, lifting one of its front legs slowly and setting it down. Then moving another leg and another.

It was coming closer.

Tessa backed against the window. She could feel the coldness of the glass seep through the back of her robe and pajamas.

The spider took another step. Now it was only about ten feet away.

What was she going to do?

The spider took another step. It was close enough now that Tessa could see the glistening moonlight reflected in its multifaceted eyes.

How could she stop it?

The only thing that had stopped it before was fire.

Fire!

Tessa reached down and felt the pack of matches in the pocket of her robe. She'd never given them back to Allie.

The spider took another step.

Tessa slid across the window. She felt the dusty curtain graze her cheek.

The curtain . . .

Moving slowly, never taking her eyes off the creature, Tessa reached up and lifted the curtain rod off the window.

The spider came closer still. Tessa slowly rolled the curtain around one end of the curtain rod.

Come on, she thought. *Come a little closer.*

Chapter 16

The spider was only four feet away now.

Tessa reached into her robe for the pack of matches.

The spider was starting to take another step.

Tessa tore off one of the matches and lit it.

The spider froze.

Tessa held the match to the balled-up curtain at the end of the curtain rod. The thin, gauzy curtain burst into flames.

The spider still hadn't moved.

Tessa jabbed the burning curtain at it, but she was too slow.

In a lightning-fast movement, the spider skittered out of reach.

Tessa stepped forward and tried to jab it again, but again the spider was too fast and jumped out of the way.

The curtain was no longer burning so brightly. In a few moments it would go out. In a last desperate attempt to drive the spider away, or kill it, or whatever, Tessa hurled the curtain rod with the burning curtain at it.

This time her aim was good. The burning ball of curtain hit the spider right in the face. There was a burst of sparks and flames as the spider was caught in the burning curtain. The spider ran away erratically, banging into pieces of furniture as it dragged the burning curtain and the curtain rod behind it.

Tessa watched, completely stunned. Had she done it? Had she actually driven the spider away—maybe even killed it? Her knees suddenly went weak, and she slid down the wall. She started to sob uncontrollably. She couldn't believe it. This incredibly horrible nightmare was over.

Too weak to stand, Tessa sat against the wall, rubbing the tears out of her eyes with the palms of her hands. She was exhausted—from lack of sleep, from hours of terror, from the thought of her dead friends.

But she couldn't help feeling glad. Somehow she'd survived. She'd never given up. There was a strange, miserable pride in that.

Then she heard a scratching sound. She looked up.

On the floor, a couple of yards away, was the spider, faint wisps of smoke rising from the spots where its fur had been scorched.

Tessa gasped and jumped up, once again backing against the cold glass of the window.

The spider moved closer, dragging one of its front legs and making that scratching sound.

There was nothing now between the spider and Tessa. The terror was a cold wave rushing through her. There was nothing she could do, no way she could fight it. This was it. It was over.

The spider took another step, dragging its bad leg behind it.

All Tessa could think about was what it had done to Sierra, Brittany, and Allie. It was a fate worse than death.

The spider took another step.

Storing up for the long cold winter . . .

Tessa pictured the large silken cocoon.

No, anything was better than that!

The spider took yet another step. A tart, acrid smell wafted toward Tessa . . . the smell of scorched spider hair.

It was only a few feet away now. Tessa could see the moonlight reflected in its many eyes. She pressed back harder against the glass.

The spider took another step. Suddenly

Tessa noticed something silvery around its neck. Like a dog collar.

Crash! The window behind Tessa finally gave way, and shrieking, she tumbled out of the attic, down, down, down.

It was a gray, cloudy dawn. Sebastian climbed up the creaking steps to the attic and opened the door.

"Fluffy?" he called. "Fluffy?"

His pet was slow to come this morning, the usual scampering sound replaced by slow, methodical thumps. Finally Fluffy appeared.

"Sweetie, what happened to you?" Sebastian asked, staring at the scorched spots in Fluffy's hair. "Poor baby." Taking the leash from his hand, he hooked one end around Fluffy's collar. Together Sebastian and Fluffy headed out of the New Arcadia on their morning walk.

Here's a sneak preview of a terrifying new series by Cynthia Blair

Dark Moon Legacy

Out on the edge of Overlook, an air of desolation hung as thick as the mist that blanketed the forest. The late-afternoon sun was barely visible against the gray sky as Miranda struggled to maneuver her bike over the narrow, pitted dirt road.

Winding Way was treacherous, an endless path of sharp turns and unexpected twists that snaked up into the hills. All around were rotted fences, jutting out from fields of weeds. Miranda hadn't been on this road since she was a child, when she and her friends used to head out on their bikes in search of adventure. She was dismayed over its state of disrepair. Yet what struck her most was the silence. Nothing, not even birds, seemed to dwell here on the outskirts of town.

But she had to see Garth. The memorial

service, Mrs. Swensen's sharp words, the terrible insinuations of Corinne and Selina . . . it had all been too much for her to bear alone. By the time the final bell rang, her desire to be with Garth had grown to a desperate longing—but she'd had no idea where to find him. She stopped in at the library, hoping that she'd see him there. He spent a lot of time doing research, so someone there might even know where he lived.

"Now, let me see," Ms. Wallace, the library clerk, had said. She'd shuffled through a box of file cards, peering through the eyeglasses she wore on a chain around her neck. "He did apply for a card recently, so I should have . . . Oh, yes, here it is. Garth Gautier . . . Winding Way."

Ms. Wallace frowned. "Hmmm. The only house I know of on Winding Way is that dilapidated old estate. What is it called? Cedar Crest?"

Miranda was startled. "Garth lives at Cedar Crest?"

Ms. Wallace shook her head. "There must be some mistake. Nobody's inhabited that old eyesore for years. I'm surprised the Board of Health hasn't had it leveled by now."

"Thanks anyway." Miranda was already halfway out the door. Now, even as she pedaled around a bend in the road and caught sight of the old house, she couldn't believe Garth really lived here. She felt sure she had

154

come all this way for nothing.

Miranda gazed up at Cedar Crest. It had always reminded her of a European castle, with its simple lines and stark landscaping. It was an elegant, L-shaped building made of pale gray stones. A tall tower joined the two wings, and along one side ran a row of French doors that opened onto the garden.

It had undoubtedly been a showplace at one time. Now, after decades of neglect, there was something forbidding about the mansion. Even in the bright afternoon light, it was shrouded in shadow. The darkened windows resembled dozens of unseeing eyes. Miranda shivered.

She leaned her bicycle against a tree and cautiously made her way toward the front door. Up close, she could see that the house was in a terrible state of decay. Many of the stones were pitted or even disintegrating. The brick path leading from the circular driveway to the front door was overgrown with weeds. She wondered if the crumbling steps would support her weight.

Miranda had to agree with Mrs. Wallace—Garth couldn't possibly live here. Still, it was the only address she had. Determined to find out, Miranda reached for the heavy brass knocker.

She was as surprised to see Garth appear at the door as he looked to see her.

"Miranda!" he said. "What are you doing here?"

"Can I come in?"

He hesitated for a moment, as if deciding, then stepped aside to let her in.

Relieved, Miranda walked into the foyer. It took a few seconds for her eyes to adjust to the darkness within. She found herself in a huge entryway. It ended at a dramatic marble staircase edged with an intricately carved wooden banister. On either side of her were cavernous rooms.

Miranda could tell that the rooms had once been elegant. Now they contained barely any furniture, the few pieces that remained obvious casualties of time. There were piles of rubble pushed into corners. Paint was peeling, decorative trim faded. And everywhere there were shadows, as if there were not enough light in the entire world to bring this place back to life.

"You shouldn't have come," Garth said woodenly. He was standing behind her as she surveyed the decrepit castle that was his home.

Miranda quickly forgot all about her bizarre surroundings. "I had to see you," she explained, turning to him.

"You don't belong here," he said in the same monotone.

"Oh, Garth, just hold me!" Unable to believe his coldness was sincere, she wrapped her arms around him and gazed up into his eyes, searching for the warmth and acceptance she craved. She desperately needed him to tell her she wasn't alone.

It seemed like an eternity before he finally clasped his arms around her, drawing her close. Miranda collapsed against his powerful chest, reveling in the sense of safety, of security, that she had yearned for.

It was like coming home.

She raised her face to his. The intensity in his blue eyes created a stirring deep inside her. Then he leaned forward, pressing his parted lips against hers. Gently at first, tentatively, as if he were asking a question. But his kiss quickly grew more ardent. Miranda eagerly gave in to it. Reaching up, she encircled his neck with her arms, her body melting against his.

Finally he drew back, nuzzling her neck. "My sweet, sweet Miranda," he whispered, his breath hot against her skin.

"Hold me," she pleaded, clinging to him. "Don't ever let go."

He grasped her even more tightly. "Oh, Miranda, what have they done to you?"

In a halting voice she told him everything. All about the memorial service for Andy Swensen. His mother's reaction to her expression of sympathy. The insensitivity of Corinne and Selina. Even her own self-doubts, her suspicion that, in some way she couldn't explain, she'd had something to do with Andy's death.

"Poor Miranda." Garth embraced her in his muscular arms, holding her as if he were desperate to infuse her with some of his own strength. "Let's forget all that for now. Let's just appreciate how wonderful it is to be together."

He took her gently by the hand and led her through the house. Miranda was breathless as she took it all in. Room after room, each more beautiful, more ornate than the last . . . all of them slipping into ruin as if they'd been cursed.

Out back was a garden. Like the rest of the house, it had obviously been lovely once. Now it was covered with weeds, the meandering paths barely visible through the stubby grass that pushed its way through. Still, Miranda could make out what had once been a rose garden, picturing it in her mind as it must have looked in late spring, alive with pink and red and yellow buds. In one corner was a fish pond, an oddly shaped pool of water that was now murky and covered with algae. Off in the distance was a maze, fashioned from shrubs that over time had become oddly misshapen. Despite its state of decline, Miranda was awestruck, and even a bit intimidated, by its grandeur.

"What a magical place!" she breathed, sinking onto a crumbling concrete bench. "How did you come to live here?"

"My family owns this estate. My grandfather built it after he made a fortune in the lumber industry." Garth glanced around with a rueful smile. "This was his reward."

"Where is he now?"

"He died a long time ago. My father had already established himself up in Portland, so he just closed it up. When I had to get out . . . when I decided to leave Portland, I came down here and opened the place up."

"Isn't it lonely, living here by yourself?" Miranda asked with concern.

A look of pain crossed Garth's face. In an even voice, he told her, "I've been alone my whole life."

They sat for a long time, hands locked together, allowing the peacefulness of the garden to settle over them. Miranda found herself telling him much of what was in her heart— the pain, the confusion, even the hope. Once again she was surprised by how easy it was being with him. Talking to him. Trusting him. Gradually a sense of peace returned.

"Let's go inside," he suggested as the sky grew darker and the gentle spring breezes became stronger. He led her back into the house, this time going off in a different direction.

They ended up in the ballroom. Miranda let out a gasp. What a magnificent room! Her eyes traveled upward, taking in the hand-carved running frieze joining the walls to the ceiling, the elaborate gold-leaf trim, the ornate cornices above the windows.

"Oh, Garth, it's gorgeous," she cried, taking his arm. "This entire house is like something out of a dream. Wouldn't it be wonderful if we could bring it alive again? We could make it just as beautiful as it was when your grandfather first built it."

She grew more excited as she imagined it. "I could work in the garden—I'll bet I could get it back into terrific shape in a single summer. And inside, we could paint and make repairs. . . ." She cast a sidelong glance at Garth, anxious to see if he was going along with her fantasy. Instead, the look on his face frightened her.

"What is it, Garth?"

"It's hearing you talk like that."

Miranda bit her lip. "I'm sorry. I didn't mean—"

"Don't you see, Miranda?" he cried. "Don't you know that's what I want too? For us to be together here? More than anything. I'd give anything if we could make it happen!"

She recoiled, taken aback by the force of his words. "Why can't we?"

"We can't see each other anymore. You must accept that."

"But I love you," she said in a quiet voice. "And . . . and I want to stay with you."

She took a step forward, her eyes locked on his, her arms held slightly toward him. With her entire body she was asking a question. Her breaths were short and quick, her chest heaving as she waited for his answer.

But instead of feeling him melt against her the way she'd hoped, she saw his muscles tense.

"No, Miranda. Don't."

"But I do love you! I can't just stop. I—I don't want to stop!"

Garth buried his face in his hands. He paced about the room, so agitated it seemed as though some other spirit had taken him over. "I was afraid of this. I tried to stop it, I thought I could control it—"

"Garth, what is it?" Miranda was confused. "Why is it wrong for me to love you? Why would I ever want to stop feeling the most wonderful feeling I've ever—"

"You don't understand." As he turned to face her, she expected to see anger in his blue eyes. Instead, she saw desperation. "I'm not what you think I am."

"But, Garth—"

"Go away, Miranda," he pleaded. "Before it's too late."

She reached up and gently placed her hand against his cheek. "It's already too late."

He moved her hand away. "Miranda, there are things about me you don't know."

"Then tell me," she pleaded. "I want to know. I want to know everything about you."

"You couldn't possibly understand—"

"I understand how I feel. I understand, for the first time in my life, what it means to love."

She took a few more steps toward him, but he drew back. He was running away from her again. He didn't want her. He knew how she felt—maybe even felt that way too, at least a little—yet he was choosing to give her up.

Suddenly a new feeling washed over her. She could feel her frustration escalating into anger.

"You're absolutely right, Garth," Miranda said. "I *don't* understand. I see that there could be something special, something wonderful between us. There already is—or at least I thought there was. But for some reason you're afraid of it. You're turning your back on it."

"Listen to me, Miranda! It's not what you think!"

"I don't know what to think. But there's one thing I do know. And that's that you're sending me away. All right; I'll go. It's not as if you're the only boy in the world who could possibly care for me."

"What are you talking about?"

A surge of power was rushing through her. She felt it was dangerous . . . yet she was already out of control, unable to stop it.

"There's someone else. Someone who pours out his heart to me in beautiful love poems. Someone who's not afraid of my love!"

She whirled around, racing toward the door of the ballroom. As she did, she heard him say her name one more time.

"Miranda!" It came out like a groan, a desperate plea.

She didn't turn back. Instead, she rushed outside into the late afternoon. The air was tinged with iciness. The approaching dusk was already painting the sky with striking reds and oranges, the towering trees darkening against the colorful backdrop.

As always, the dramatic landscape reminded her that she was but one small part of a universe so great and so powerful that it was impossible to fathom. But her own pain was so wrenching, her feelings of loss so great, her hopelessness so devastating, that this time there was no comfort even in that thought.

Once again the moon was full.

The autumn night was biting, winter's icy fingers already gripping the forest.

Tonight, he was not part of the night.

Instead, he gazed out the window, narrow panes crisscrossed with iron bars.

He had imprisoned himself purposely. Earlier that evening, he had waited inside

Cedar Crest, agonizing over his fate . . . wondering if perhaps he could alter it.

He knew that the change would come upon him tonight. That once again the beast would be unable to resist its evil nature. Yet he was determined to fight the desire to seek out human flesh. And so when night began to fall, he had descended into the depths of Cedar Crest, where his only weapon against total blackness was a single hurricane lamp. He watched as its pale flame cast long shadows upon the crumbling stone steps and the narrow twisting hallways.

Down in the cellar, among the thick cobwebs, nestled between the now-empty wine cellar and the abandoned storage areas, was a small room. He had been inside only once, puzzling over its purpose.

Now he understood.

It was a prison of sorts, a cell in which someone—or something—could be locked away, unable to cause harm. The only window was barred. The door was thick wood, so warped that it was wedged firmly into the concrete frame.

The lock was on the outside.

He wasn't sure his plan would work, but he had to try. If only this room could contain him while the moon was full! If only it could enforce a control that he himself lacked.

If only this room would keep the werewolf from killing again.

When the moon began to rise, he had come inside, pushing hard against the door, confident that even the strongest animal would be unable to find a way of getting past it.

Now he waited.

Staring out the window, he watched the moon rise, and felt the change begin. It started with a tingling sensation that electrified his skin. His jaw lengthened, his muscles swelled, fine golden hairs sprouted everywhere. He watched with great curiosity, anxious to see how the beast would react.

Gradually the boy's awareness faded. Once again the beast emerged.

At first it was confused. It blinked, unable to comprehend the four gray walls that surrounded it, containing it inside such a small space.

It grew more agitated as it paced, sniffing the walls, searching for a means of escape. It yearned to test its muscles to the limit, to race through the forest. Its senses were as sharp as always, its nostrils flaring as it tried to pick out anything familiar, its ears pricked in an attempt at discovering what this place was.

And then, the rage.

Never before had the beast been contained. Never before had its instinctive drive to roam freely through the forest been restrained. Never before had its urge to hunt been crushed.

The beast raised its head to release an agonized howl of defeat.

Then it heard the voices.

"Are you sure about this, Corinne?"

"What are you, Paul, chicken?"

Two boys. They spoke in whispers, their voices edged with fear. The beast froze, its senses even more alert than before.

"Come on, Tommy. Don't back out on us now. You promised, remember?"

A girl, this time.

"Besides, it's only a practical joke. Paul's idea about shooting off firecrackers was a brainstorm."

"Yeah, but you'd better keep your voice down, Corinne. Otherwise the only surprise around here is gonna be Miranda's boyfriend coming after us with a baseball bat."

The beast heard their words without understanding them. What it did understand was that the three voices were right outside the basement window, coming closer every second.

The urge to hunt was overwhelming.

"How are we supposed to get in?" demanded one of the boys. "The front door's locked."

"Are you guys for real?" The girl's tone was one of exasperation. "We'll break in through the basement. There's probably a door somewhere."

166

There was a long silence. "I don't know, Corinne," said one of the boys. "That's breaking and entering. Not exactly the same thing as a practical joke."

"You are afraid, aren't you? Well, who needs you? I can do this myself."

"Let's go back, Corinne." The boy sounded even more afraid than before. "Maybe this wasn't such a good idea, after all."

"You go. I can manage. Give me that flashlight."

The beast watched through the window, taking care to stay in the shadows. Every muscle was tense. It longed to strike out, to break through the glass. Yet something inside told it to hold back—to hide in the darkness and wait.

The three of them argued some more, gradually moving out of the beast's range. Once again it began its agitated pacing. It leaped up against the cold stone walls, its head nearly reaching the ceiling. There was no way out. Anxiously it circled the small space, desperate to escape. And then it froze.

It heard a noise.

It pointed its ears upward. Someone was rattling the rotted wooden door at the end of the corridor.

From the scent, the beast knew it was the girl.

And then she was inside the house.

"I knew it," she muttered. "An old wreck like this is bound to be easy to get into. Now all I need is a place to light these stupid firecrackers."

The beast stood perfectly still. It lurked in the shadowy space next to the door, prepared to pounce. Its nose twitched as the scent of the girl grew stronger.

She was moving closer.

And then, "Are you nuts, Corinne? Let's get out of here!"

One of the boys had come back.

"Look, Paul. I've come this far—"

"If you get caught, you're dead! Come on! It's not worth it."

"Oh, all right. You go ahead with Tommy. I'll catch up with you in a minute."

"Do what you want, but Tommy and I are outta here."

Her scent was growing weaker. She was moving away. The beast relaxed its stance, lying on the cold stone floor in defeat. It could hear her moving down the corridor uncertainly.

The footsteps stopped. For a long time, there was silence. The beast waited, ears pricked, not yet ready to give up.

And then the sound resumed, this time taking a different direction. Suddenly her scent flooded the room. She was pushing against the door.

Instantly the beast was poised. With a great creaking sound, the wooden door moved. In the dim light it saw her silhouette in the doorway.

She paused, blinking. And then, catching sight of the huge form crouching before her, she let out a piercing scream. She turned and ran, racing through the winding corridor. The beast followed. Its massive form was an encumbrance here in the narrow hallways, its movements slowed down by the slippery floor, the unexpected turns, the unfamiliar space in which even its keen senses could not help it find its way.

And then it was outdoors. The girl was rushing toward the woods, her gasping breaths filled with fear. The beast raced after her, loping across the fields, its urge to hunt stronger than ever.

Finally it reached the forest. Out here, no living creature could match the beast's speed. None could match its power.

None could match its determination.

Easily it reached the girl, catching up with her in a small clearing. She turned, a look of horror on her face, too terrified even to scream.

A glorious feeling of release washed over the beast. It stood poised for only a moment. And then it pounced, meeting with little resistance as it shoved its victim to the ground.

1 (800) I LUV BKS!

If you'd like to hear more about your
favorite young adult novels and writers . . .
OR
If you'd like to tell us what you thought
of this book or other books
you've recently read . . .

CALL US at 1(800) I LUV BKS
[1(800)458-8257]

You'll hear a new message about books and
other interesting subjects each month.

**The call is free to you, but please get
your parents' permission first.**